BALLYVAUGHAN

AN EDDIE HOLLAND NOVEL

JOHN H. MATTHEWS

Ballyvaughan
Written by John H. Matthews
Copyright © 2015 by John H. Matthews

ISBN: 978-0-9897233-2-9

This is a work of fiction. Names, characters, places, and
incidents either are the product of the author's imagination or
are used fictitiously, and any resemblance to actual persons,
living or dead, business establishments, events or locales is
entirely coincidental. No Volkswagens were injured in
the writing of this book.

Bluebullseye Press
www.bluebullseyepress.com
A division of Bluebullseye LLC

Edited by Ginger Moran

Cover photo and design
Copyright © 2015 John H. Matthews

Author photo courtesy
Kevin Davis Photography

*For Brennan
though I won't let him read it
for another eighteen years.*

CHAPTER 1

Eddie's back was against the light green cement block wall. His Glock 19 nine-millimeter pistol was in his hand and aimed towards the ground. He felt his cell phone vibrate in his shirt pocket, pressed into his chest by the bulletproof vest he had taken from the trunk of a police car outside. He hated wearing vests, but hated the idea of being dead worse.

He reached the corner to the main hallway lined with gunmetal grey lockers, lowered to one knee and looked quickly around the edge to get a look down the deserted hall.

At the far end was a man on the floor, and even from

a distance Eddie could see a small pool of blood that had gathered around the figure and no body movement. The officers outside had told him that one person had been reported shot. He could hear a few sounds from classrooms on either side of the hall where students were likely hidden behind overturned desks, their teachers protecting them as best they could. But it was the cafeteria Eddie was looking for, where the 911 call had come from.

The cell phone vibrated again. Eddie knew it was Gus calling from outside the single story school where he was standing with the other police officers to yell at him. He dug under the top of the vest and pulled the phone out and answered.

"Not a good time," Eddie said.

"What the hell are you doing?" Gus Ramirez said..

"A bunch of cruisers sped past me with lights and sirens and I followed to see what was up. I got kinda bored out there with all the local PD," Eddie said. "You know Sergeant Kincaid had a kid last week?"

"Yes, I do," Gus said. "I sent flowers."

"Flowers?" Eddie said. "What's a baby going to do with flowers?"

"Would you get out here right now?" Gus said.

"Nah. I think I'll look around some more," Eddie

said. "Why are you here, anyway?"

"The police chief called me," Gus said. "He asked for Bureau assistance in case the hostage rescue team is needed. Now get out. SWAT is minutes out."

"No can do, old friend. We both know how these things end when SWAT gets involved," Eddie said. "They'll throw a couple of flashbangs, run through the smoke with guns raised and some kid or teacher gets shot."

He could hear Gus tapping his phone against his forehead, frustrated with Eddie.

"Well, what do you see in there," Gus said.

"There's a man down at the north end of the hallway. There's some blood on the floor under him," Eddie said.

"Probably the principal," Gus said. "According to the caller he's the only one who's been shot. Let's hope he's the only one at least."

"Stay with me," Eddie said. "I'm going in for a better look."

He pushed the cellphone into the back pocket of his jeans without disconnecting then took another look down the hall. Stepping away from the relative safety of the wall he turned left and ran towards the end of the hallway, thankful for his well-worn running shoes he'd pulled on that morning that kept his steps muffled.

A set of steel doors with a narrow glass panel on each were closed at the end of the hall and Eddie came to a stop with his back to the door on the right. The body of the school's principal lay a few feet away. Eddie reached and placed two fingers on the man's neck then pulled his hand away. He took the phone out of his pocket.

"Principal is dead," Eddie said.

"That's not good news," Gus said. "PD is itching to breach and that'll make it worse."

"Just hold them off," Eddie said. "Get me a few more minutes. Don't tell them about the principal yet."

"Hold off SWAT?" Gus said. "I'll get right on that. Just hurry. But be careful."

"Which is it, hurry or be careful?" Eddie said.

"Shut up," Gus said.

Eddie leaned against the door and looked at the motionless man in front of him. It was far from the first time he'd seen a dead body, but the sight always hit something inside him. He glanced at the man's left hand and saw no ring, which relieved him. He shook off the emotions he was feeling and looked around him.

"I smell tater-tots," Eddie said.

"How do you know they're tater-tots and not French fries?" Gus said.

"I just know," Eddie said.

"Guess you found the cafeteria then," Gus said. "Do you have a visual on the shooter?"

Eddie kept low on his feet and turned to look through the window. In the far corner of the large room there was at least 30 children huddled together, with a few adults holding them back trying to keep them calm. He tried to see the rest of the room but the skinny window kept his field of vision limited.

"A few dozen kids and some teachers in the far corner away from the windows," Eddie said. "No visual on the shooter. I'm going to try to find a better angle."

The phone back in his pocket, he looked into the room again and saw the counters at the back of the cafeteria where the students were served their lunches each day. He moved away from the door then ran down the side hallway to find a way into the kitchen. He tried two doors, which turned out to be the teacher's lounge and a broom closet. The third door opened to a narrow hallway where the smell of a commercial kitchen was strong.

At the end of the hallway was a closed door with no windows. With no other choices, he turned the knob and pulled it open a couple of inches and looked through. He could see two women in white aprons and hairnets lying on the floor, one with a cell phone to her ear.

Eddie moved into the room and lowered to the ground. The women saw him and he motioned them to be silent as he worked his way to the counter.

"All of you just shut the hell up," a voice yelled in the cafeteria. "I'm tired of you telling me what to do."

Eddie listened to the shooter talking and waited. A woman's voice came next.

"Adrian, please," she said. "Let the kids go. Just keep the teachers-"

The sound of a shotgun getting cocked, a shell being brought into chamber, silenced the woman. Eddie moved in a crouched position to the far corner of the serving window where he felt the shooter couldn't see him and stood up. He was only ten feet from the children and teachers huddled in the corner. He knew if any of them reacted to him standing there the situation could get much worse.

He just needed a general idea of where in the room the shooter was. He locked eyes with one of the teachers that were holding the children back. Eddie nodded his head in the direction he thought the shooter was from him. The man moved his eyes into the room then back at Eddie and gave the slightest nod.

Taking a deep breath he looked around the edge of the opening, only exposing enough of his head for him to get a good look at the shooter and the room around him then pulled back. He liked what he saw.

The far wall was lined with windows but they were all covered with white plastic to deflect the hot Austin sun. The shooter looked to be a teenage boy and he was looking through an open window at the dozens of law enforcement that were gathered outside, eager to meet him.

With his gun moved to his left hand momentarily, Eddie used his right hand for support and threw his legs over the counter on the short wall into the main cafeteria. He knew he only had a few seconds before students started reacting and alerted the shooter.

Both feet on the linoleum floor and gun back in his right hand, raised and aimed at the shooter, Eddie worked to close the 40 foot distance as fast as he could. He knew the closer he got the better chance he had of taking the shooter with one shot if he had to, but also the boy would have a much better shot at Eddie with the wide spray of the 12-guage shotgun.

He was 20 feet away from his target before a child behind him shrieked. The teen turned his head and saw Eddie closing in on him with the pistol aimed at his chest. The shotgun was still pointed to the floor. The boy looked down at the shotgun and back to Eddie.

Eddie stopped, his gun still aimed at the boy.

"I wouldn't do that. I'll shoot you before you have a chance to pull the trigger," Eddie said.

"I'm already dead," the boy said. "I'll get the chair."

"You mean for the principal? He's alive, for now." Eddie lied. "You can still walk out of here. But let's not scar these kids any more than we have to. There's a chance a few may still turn out somewhat normal, even after this."

"What is normal?" The boy looked at the kids, smiled, then began to raise the shotgun towards Eddie.

Eddie ran towards the teen and the shotgun that was now aimed at him. He pulled his aim slightly to the right and began squeezing the trigger on his pistol while closing the distance. He kept pulling the trigger and the bullets flew past the teenager and struck the cement wall below the windows. The sound of the shots was loud in the concrete and tiled cafeteria and the teen reacted to the blast of the gun firing at him and turned away, the shotgun's aim dropping. Eddie lowered his weapon and sprinted the last few feet and tackled the boy, pinning his arms to his sides, his head smashed into the cold floor. He turned the boy over, face down on the floor.

"Clear!" Eddie yelled. He kicked the shotgun away and checked the boy for any other weapons while still holding him face down on the ground. He knew SWAT would enter the school as soon as his shots were heard.

The main cafeteria doors burst open and a dozen members of the SWAT team stormed in, M-4 assault rifles raised as they spread through the room. Two of the officers came and took Eddie's place and within moments had handcuffs around the shooter's wrists and ankles.

Eddie checked his weapon, cleared the chamber and placed it back in the holster in the small of his back then ripped the Velcro straps of the bulletproof vest off and tossed it to the floor.

"What the hell were you thinking?" Gus Ramirez came through the door and moved towards Eddie.

"I was thinking I could avoid another Columbine or Sandy Hook," Eddie said. "The officers hands were tied waiting for SWAT to make the situation go from bad to worse. I made a decision to get in here and stop it."

Gus shook his head.

"You weren't thinking," Gus said. "You aren't a cop. You're not an agent anymore. You haven't even filed for your private detective's license yet. What if this hadn't worked out the way it had?"

"But it did," Eddie said.

CHAPTER 2

A ran Driscoll sat at the bar, a pint of beer held between his hands. His eyes were on the thick, dark liquid as the bubbles defied logic and gravity and moved from the surface down the inside of the glass towards the bottom. He'd heard once why the bubbles did this, but he couldn't recall so he took another drink.

He had been in Ballyvaughan just under 18 months and wasn't on a first name basis, or any name basis, with the barkeep who poured him a pint every afternoon or the woman who checked his groceries out in the store across the road. The old man he rented his apartment from hadn't even asked for identification after he'd paid cash for a year in advance when he first let the flat over the owner's store on the main street, then again when the informal lease came up. Aran didn't even balk at the ten extra euros a month the man wanted the second time around.

He stood and reached into his pocket to pay for the beer. He'd stopped carrying a wallet years before. A simple sliver clip with whatever paper money he needed avoided having anything personal on him, anything that could identify him. He had no real driver's license in any country and the stack of fake licenses and passports hidden in a loose stone on the right side of the fireplace in his mother's home all held other men's names and nationalities. He'd passed as Scottish, British, American and Canadian, and one time even went easily through customs in Austria with a passport from Russia.

His tab paid, he stood and left without bothering to wave at the owner of the bar as everyone else did when leaving. He glanced to his right then stepped into the road and walked across to the small café that advertised "internet access" in the window. He gave the teenage girl behind the counter enough money for a few minutes of time on the Internet. He sat down at one of the two outdated computers. The large monitor took up most of the table, barely leaving room for the keyboard. He glanced around to make sure nobody was watching and then opened the website where he received his email.

The list of messages was a who's who of spam with no personal notes in the dozen or so that had come in since Aran had last checked the week before. He selected each message promoting home loans, sales at stores he'd never heard of, sure-fire weight loss tips and turning your paycheck into a fortune and clicked the "delete" icon. His mouse moved up to the corner to close the browser when a new message appeared in the empty inbox he'd just cleared. A muted ping sounded from the decade old machine that sat under the table.

He glanced behind himself once more then opened the message. The sender was a generic email address that looked like more spam, but it was the only person Aran ever awaited messages from. The body of the email contained only a short sentence and a link.

The message said "This is the man you are looking for."

He clicked the link and watched as a new window opened and the CNN website came up. A video began to play a story from the day before about a school shooting in Austin, Texas and the hero of the day who had refused to be interviewed on camera. No sound came from the computer, but the news report had enough text at the bottom of the screen for Aran to follow along. The reporter pointed the man out in the background as the cameraman zoomed in to show the hero standing and talking with a group of men in suits and uniforms.

Aran clicked and paused the video. The face of Eddie Holland filled the screen. He then clicked the button to write a reply and typed a single sentence, "Make the arrangements," and sent the email.

He pointed the mouse up to the menu at the top of the browser and went through the few steps to erase the history, and then quit the browser and turned the computer off to clear the memory then quietly left the cafe.

Ballyvaughan sits on the edge of the Atlantic Ocean, with only his namesake islands between the cobblestone streets and wide-open waters. Aran pulled his collar up and moved into the wind to walk the half-mile distance to the two-room house on the edge of town.

He got to the door and pressed down on the latch with his thumb and it didn't give.

"Shite," he muttered. "Not again."

He knocked on the door, gently at first and then louder until he heard movement inside.

They had moved into the house just before Aran was born and it was seven years later that his father left them. His mother never spoke of him again and Aran had learned not to ask.

He'd spent his first few months back in Ballyvaughan watching her from a distance, afraid to approach her. Once he saw the signs of her weakness, he knew he had to see her. He still lived in his apartment on the main street but spent most of his time at her home.

"Who is it?" her frail voice came through the door.

"Ma, it's me. It's Aran."

Maura Driscoll opened the door and stared at her son and for a moment he didn't think she recognized him, which wouldn't have been the first time. He reached out and took her by the arm and led her to the chair she would spend her days and evenings in. The room was cold and he put more wood on the dying fire and stoked it until flames were going up inside the chimney.

The house was simple and looked exactly as it had when he'd left more than 25 years before. He sat down in the chair facing his mother and looked around the room. The small bed he'd slept on as a child was still under the window.

One night after dinner when he was 16 he sat and waited for two hours until she finally tried to kiss his forehead as he pulled away then she went to her bedroom, the only other room in the tiny house. Aran lay down on the small cot in the corner of the main room and listened for sounds from the other side of the wooden door that separated him from her bedroom.

When he was younger he'd hear crying from her room. He'd put his pillow over his head and try to ignore it. But as the years went on after her husband left, it just became silence as she went off to sleep. She never remarried.

Still dressed in his clothes from the day, he'd stepped out of bed and rolled his blanket up into a bindle with a few supplies from the kitchen he'd stowed under his mattress over the last few days, some bread, jam, and a sausage. He put a few pieces of silverware in and a large kitchen knife, more for protection than eating, he thought. He went to the fireplace and pulled a loose stone from the right side and took out a small stack of money and replaced the stone. He'd taken money from his mother's purse over the last several weeks and had saved everything he'd earned from small jobs around town as well as betting on himself in fights behind the school.

He'd opened the door then stood on the other side and for a moment didn't know what to do. He'd planned this for what seemed like years, but it had been only a few months. The small town that had become so claustrophobic to him was now the first obstacle he had to overcome. For a brief moment he considered going back inside, climbing in his bed and just forgetting all about his plan. But he shook off the feeling and took his first step away from his home and his mother.

Over the years leading up to his leaving he'd watched as she read the newspaper every morning, always reading updates on the fighting in Northern Ireland. When Aran would ask her about it she would brush him off, and just tell him it was grown up matters.

Aran had plenty of time alone in the small house while his mother worked. He'd gone through her room and found a stack of articles about the Troubles, and about how it all began with a riot in the Bogside in Derry. At the bottom of the stack was a clipping of an announcement of the marriage between two Derry residents, Declan Driscoll and Maura O'Connell.

Once he knew where his parents were from, he understood more about the way his mother reacted to reading the news. And the more he thought about it the more he knew where he wanted to be, where he needed to be, and where his father was.

Four months earlier he had asked her if his father was fighting the British, if he was IRA. She told him to never ask about that again and to forget about his father. From that point on he learned what he could about the conflicts, reading the paper after his mother went to bed.

He moved in the darkness through the small town, each step taking him further from the only life he'd known. He traded the certainty of a mother who loved him for the uncertainty of a father he didn't even know was alive or not.

He'd spent what felt to be another lifetime away from this place, fighting the British then killing for money. He looked at the old woman in front of him, her health deteriorating and her memory fading. He'd planned to stay here and be by her side until the end, it was the least he could do after deserting her for the better part of three decades, but that had changed with the message he'd received.

Now he knew the name of the man who had killed his father and he knew where to find him.

CHAPTER 3

"Y ou did a good thing," Eva said.

"Thanks," Eddie said. "Gus doesn't see it that way. Not yet, at least."

"As long as you two have known each other, this is not going to be the end of the world," Eva said. "There's surely things you've done that pissed him off more than this?"

"I wrecked his first car in high school," Eddie said. "He'd worked two summers to raise the money for it."

"See? And he got over it, didn't he?"

"I don't really think so," Eddie said.

They sat with cold drinks in their hands on the back

patio of the restaurant in Hyde Park neighborhood of Austin where they'd had their first date nearly a year earlier. He was on his second beer and she had nursed a margarita so long the ice was mostly melted. She had slept all day after rolling off three straight nights of 12 hour shifts in the emergency room before Eddie finally talked her into going out for dinner.

Eva had finished her residency at the hospital in Austin after medical school in Houston. She had just been brought on full time when Eddie Holland ended up as her patient in the emergency room after being hit on the head with a lead ball sap twelve months earlier.

"If I know Gus, and I think I do since you two are evidently a package deal, he'll be fine. Just give him some time," Eva said. "Maybe he just wishes he'd been the one to go into that school, to be the hero."

"Unlikely," Eddie said. "He's always been very by-the-book, especially with career choices to think about."

"Is he going to leave Austin?" Eva said.

"He doesn't want to. But if he's going to be promoted he has to go to a field office or DC," Eddie said. "San Antonio would be his first choice of course, but the Special Agent in Charge down there seems quite comfortable."

"He'll figure it out," Eva said.

"I hope so. It would be hard to leave you if Gus and I move to another city," Eddie said.

Eva threw her napkin across the table, hitting Eddie in the face.

"And what about you?" Eva said. "You've been stringing Gus and the FBI on for a long time now. Think you'll ever go back full time?"

Eddie took a long drink from his beer and motioned to the waitress walking by for another.

"Need one more if conversation is going to turn heavy," Eddie said.

"Don't mean to make it heavy, just practical," Eva said. "You talk about Gus leaving, but if you went back you definitely wouldn't be assigned to Austin or San Antonio."

"No, I wouldn't," Eddie said. "I'd be back in the windowless rooms of nameless buildings in Northern Virginia."

"You make it sound so exciting," Eva said.

"It's quite glamorous," Eddie said. "Bad coffee from machines in hallways, overbearing young agents trying to make a name for themselves. Then there's the guys from the Agency. God, I don't miss them."

"You like your life now?" Eva said.

"Again, heavy," Eddie said. "And yes, I do. I get to

work with people, not just data and intel from sources around the world, but still get to stay connected to the Bureau without pulling 80 hour work weeks. But it's also all I know. It was my dream, my mission, from high school on. And I made it. Now I'm not so sure. I just don't know what the next chapter would be."

"You like helping people, being a private detective," she said.

"I do. But is it really sustainable? Is that a living?" Eddie said. "And there's you, of course."

"Oh, I'm blushing, you sweet talker," Eva said.

He wanted to ask her now, here, but wasn't ready. This was the longest relationship Eddie had been in since high school. He didn't want to screw it up.

"How about you?" he said. "Is it Austin for life?"

"I love it here," Eva said. "But I'm not from here. I could go if I needed, and I can stay if I'm needed."

CHAPTER 4

A glass of Green Spot whiskey in his hand, he watched the flames dance and try to lull him to sleep. Too many nights of his life had been spent on the hard ground or in houses that should have fallen years earlier for him to sleep well anymore. A finger or two of whiskey would usually take enough of the edge off for him to fade away for a few hours rest.

He wished to be back in Belfast, to feel the spirits of Michael Collins and Bobby Sands on the streets he had walked and fought on. But the Belfast he'd left behind was different than it was now. Even though they had ended more than 20 years ago, the Troubles had left it a lost city, struggling to find an identity that didn't involve the shootings and bombings that marked headlines across the United Kingdom, Europe and further. Walls and barbed wire still separate the Catholic and Protestant neighborhoods.

Walls covered in murals of long dead heroes had become tourist attractions for travelers from other nations who knew little of what had transpired between Northern Ireland and England for more than three decades. The riot in the Bogside that erupted the Troubles was now a short page in a history book and mostly forgotten outside the country.

He heard the click of the latch on her bedroom door and turned to see his mother move through the room and sit across from him, as they had done most of the time he was there. She motioned to the bottle of whisky and he poured a short glass and handed it to her. Her face showed the expression of someone wanting to talk, not listen.

"We'd been married only a few months and were still living in my parents house," Maura said. "We couldn't afford our own place yet."

Aran set his glass down on the table. She was more coherent than he'd seen her in for quite some time.

"I was 19 and Declan, oh, he would have been 21,"

her gaze turned from the fireplace to Aran. "Do you know about the Bogside?"

"Yes, Ma," he said.

"Declan had stood and marched with his brothers and was there when the men from the British army killed all of those boys and men during the riot in the Bogside. It was supposed to be a peaceful protest. England had arrested and held hundreds of our people under suspicion of being IRA," she sipped from the whisky. "He had stayed away from any involvement until that day. But after the bloodshed he didn't hesitate any longer and joined the line of men ready to fight."

She'd never spoken about his father. To hear her now speak so openly was foreign.

"Then one night while we were lying in our bed I told him," she said. "I told him I was pregnant. He just stared at me, right in the eyes. I didn't know whether he was happy or upset, then he pulled me in tight. He told me we were going to get out of there. He said we're leavin' and I know just where we'll go.

"It was only a few nights later. We didn't even leave a note for my parents. We just left in the middle of the night. He'd taken a car from a few streets over and we put whatever we could into it and just left," she dabbed her eyes with the handkerchief in the pocket of her robe.

"He drove and drove. Whenever I'd ask him where we were goin' he would just tell me to rest, to take care of our boy. Even then he was sure it was a boy."

A log in the fire gave way and broke into several pieces, splitting the flame in two. Aran stood and put a new piece of wood on top then moved it around with the iron poker.

"I woke up and realized the car was stopped and it was morning," Maura said. "I looked out and saw him standing there, the ocean in front of him, water coming right up to his feet. I don't think I ever loved him more than I did in that moment. I'd only seen the ocean once when I was little, even though it wasn't far from Derry, but this was different. It was endless. I went to him and he told me it was our new home. He'd brought me to Ballyvaughan. He held me and we watched the water. He pointed out to the low islands and told me, 'that's the Aran Islands.' And I knew."

CHAPTER 5

E ddie drove through downtown Austin to meet a new client. His leave of absence was still in place with the FBI and he took small detective jobs when they came around, as well as acting as a special consultant to the FBI's Austin office that his oldest friend Gus Ramierez now ran. He had spent more than ten years following the events of September 11th, 2001, working counter terrorism in Washington, D.C. and had burned out on the eighteen-hour days with no breaks.

He pulled the Karmann Ghia into an empty parking space in front of Our Sister of Heavenly Grace Catholic Church just north of the University of Texas campus.

The parking lot was empty on a Tuesday morning except for the bright blue Chevrolet Cruze compact sedan that belonged to the church's leader.

Out of his car and through the front door of the mission style building, Eddie stopped at the back of the rows of pews where the parishioners sat and knelt and prayed.

Eddie was always uncomfortable in churches and today was no exception, unable to understand the concept of blind faith. He needed something tangible, something more defined, something more reciprocal. He believed in the law, which could be argued was more confusing than religion at times. He believed in his gun. He believed in his life-long friendship with Gus. He believed in his love for his sister and her two children. And now he believed in Eva Taylor and their growing relationship.

"Ten feet in the door and you haven't been struck by lightning yet," a voice came from behind him.

Eddie lowered his head and grinned then turned to greet the man.

"Eddie, I'm glad you made it," the man said.

"No way I wouldn't, Padre."

He never had called the man Father, not out of disrespect but out of his own dislike of being judged.

"Any chance you'll join your sister and her family to a mass?" the priest said.

Father Domenic Paul wore jeans and a black shirt with the stiff white collar wrapped around his neck. He always joked that his parents had decided he would be a priest at birth when they gave him his name.

"Well," Eddie said. "I…"

"Stop it, Eddie," Father Domenic said. "I know better. It isn't my style to pressure anyone into coming to church. Shelley keeps asking me to, but I know you and I know it just isn't going to happen. Now I can at least tell her I tried."

"It isn't because I don't like you," Eddie said.

"It isn't for everyone, I know that," Father Domenic said. "Now I hope you know I didn't call you here to make you uncomfortable."

Eddie smiled an awkward smile, always surprised at the pious man's incredible understanding of human behavior, especially his.

"I would like to hire you," Father Domenic said. "I went to your sister, figuring her law firm uses private detectives at times and she said you do some work for them and I couldn't think of anyone I would trust more."

"I appreciate it, Padre," Eddie said.

"You know, Eddie," Father Dominic said, "You can call me Domenic, or Dom, if you prefer."

"I didn't mean to offend you," Eddie said.

"No offense taken, I actually like Padre," Domenic said. "It's the closest thing I've ever had to a nickname and priests rarely ever get nicknames, at least not ones that are said to their faces."

They both laughed and Eddie relaxed more than he ever had inside a house of worship, including when he stood at the front of this very church when he was made godfather for his nephew Shane at the christening ten years ago. The priest standing before him allowed Eddie to fill the role generally reserved for confirmed Catholics.

The two men walked past the pews at Dominic's lead and into the back office. The priest always gave the office staff Tuesday mornings off after the busy Sunday services then the Monday morning business dealing with the donations that had come in over the weekend. They sat down across from each other in his private office after Father Domenic had poured coffee for both of them.

"So what I can do for you?" Eddie said.

"It's my niece," Domenic said. "It seems she has a stalker."

"That can be serious," Eddie said. "Has she had any threats or feel in danger?"

"No, so far the notes have been mostly adoring," Domenic said. "She's a musician and singer and has been getting a lot of attention from record labels."

"Good for her," Eddie said.

"This man thinks her songs are written for him," Domenic said. "He writes to her and tells her he feels the same way for her. But she sang a song at a performance a week or so ago, a new song about breaking up."

"And he thought it was directed towards him?" Eddie said.

"Exactly," Domenic said.

"I'd be happy to help. Tell me how to get a hold of her," Eddie said.

"Her name is Mary Simon but she goes by Mari, like calamari," Domenic said. The priest handed Eddie a note card with Mari's name and phone number.

"Mari? Not stuck on being a traditional Catholic I guess," Eddie said.

"Far from it. She's always pushing me to get the church 'caught up to the twenty-first century,' like I have any say in it."

Eddie grinned and flipped the card between his fingers.

"Is she expecting me?" Eddie said.

"I told her I wanted to get someone to help her. She resisted at first, but after the last note over the break up song, she changed her mind," Domenic said. "Her parents live in Dallas and my sister counts on me to keep an eye on her."

"You're a good brother," Eddie said with the intended pun.

"Nice one," Domenic said.

CHAPTER 6

The bus pulled up to the international departures terminal at Shannon airport and Aran Driscoll stepped off, a small black leather bag his only luggage. He wore jeans and a dress shirt with the tails out and a khaki sports coat from a tailor in Belfast. He was handsome in an unrefined way, his hair always a little messy and stubble on his face and just attractive enough not to be noticed when he didn't want to be. Inside the building he stopped at one of the overpriced convenience shops and bought a disposable phone. Once out of the shop, he turned the phone on and sent a blank text to a phone number he knew from memory, then went to the airport bar and ordered a beer.

He watched the televisions over the rows of liquor bottles as he drank. After fifteen minutes the phone beeped, he looked at the screen and read the one word that appeared: Dallas.

After paying the tab for the beer he walked to the ticket counter and bought a one-way ticket to Dallas, Texas by way of JFK airport in New York City. With three hours before the flight, he returned to the bar and ordered another beer.

CHAPTER 7

Running shirtless as always, the cool fall air bristled his skin but once he was at speed and warmed up he felt good. It was mid-afternoon and the sun was shining and the temperature held steady in the low 60s.

With plenty of time on his hands that afternoon he turned left at the end of his block and headed for the trail that led towards downtown two miles away. Twelve minutes later he ran along Town Lake across from the busy metropolitan center of the small city. Zilker Park was almost empty and he had the trails mostly to himself, the luxury of running on a weekday when the business people were working and the musicians and artists were still sleeping. A few moms pushed jogging strollers with large bicycle tires in back that took up most of the trail.

Austin is an anomaly, a blue dot in a red sea. The capitol of a notoriously right-leaning state is a stronghold of liberal thinking creative types. Discussions over drinks are more likely to be about the latest local bands than what was happening at the large capitol building a few blocks from 6th street.

Eddie continued southeast along Lady Bird Lake Trail and crossed the footbridge that kept pedestrians off of the busier Barton Springs Road Bridge. A short while later he passed the Stevie Ray Vaughn statue that faced downtown over Town Lake. He glanced to his right at the tree where he had been knocked unconscious almost a year earlier while working a case and kept going, picking up his pace to prove to no one but himself that he could still do so. He'd put his sister and her family in danger that time and hoped to never let that happen again.

By the time he returned home he had run more than thirteen miles and could have easily doubled it to make a marathon distance. He showered and dressed himself in blue jeans and an FBI Athletic Department tee shirt he'd bought from a street vendor in Washington, D.C. and a corduroy sports coat on top of it. His gun stayed in its mahogany box in the nightstand beside his bed. He grabbed his porkpie hat with the small orange feather on the left side and left the apartment.

At 6:15 he parked on the street in front of Buddy's Music Saloon on the west end of the seven block strip of 6th Street where all of the bars and clubs lined the road. As he opened the door the music spilled out into the street, an acoustic guitar and a woman's voice matched in tone and beauty. He paused for a moment to watch Mari Simon as she went through a sound check for that night's show.

The owner of the club walked over to Eddie.

"Pretty good, isn't she?"

"Sure sounds like it, Buddy," Eddie and the man shook hands and leaned in for the masculine version of a hug, their right shoulders bumping then leaning back out. The two men had gone to high school together, the bar owner a year ahead of Eddie but on the same football team that had gone to the state championships only to lose to a team from Wichita Falls.

"How's business?" Eddie said.

"Can't complain," Buddy said. "Recessions never seem to affect live music and good liquor much."

"Good to hear," Eddie said. "What do you know

about this girl?"

"I know she's a bit young for you," Buddy said.

"Nah, nothing like that," Eddie said. "I've been asked to check into a situation she's in."

"You mean the notes?" Buddy said.

"You know about them?" Eddie said.

"Sure, a lot of them have been delivered to the bar. She plays here a couple times a week," Buddy said.

"You have security cameras?" Eddie said.

"Sure don't. We get more of the music lover's crowd that happens to drink rather than the drinking crowds that talk over the music and get themselves into trouble. We've never needed cameras." Buddy said.

"No problem," Eddie said. "I'm going to go listen in then talk to her when she's done."

"Shouldn't be long, she likes to do a solo song or two then a full band number to get the sound right," Buddy said. "She's a bit of a perfectionist."

"Sounds like it pays off," Eddie said.

Eddie sat at one of the raised round tables in the back of the club and listened to Mari Simon sing. She finished up a song with her acoustic guitar and the rest of her band came onto the stage. She traded her guitar for a mandolin, ran her finger down the strings to check the tuning, and looked back at the drummer as she tapped her heel four times to lead the percussionist into the beat. The guitar and bass players followed and entered the song seamlessly.

The music that came out of them was far better than a college town bar band, even by Austin's standards. The high notes of the mandolin floated the melody over the electric guitar as the drummer kept a smooth tempo without ever overwhelming the stringed instruments. Then Mari turned to the microphone and began to sing and the skin on Eddie's arms vibrated. Her voice was an extension of the music.

Without even listening to the lyrics Eddie immediately knew how someone could think she was singing directly to him and was surprised she didn't have dozens of stalkers instead of just one.

The song ended and Eddie wanted to hear more.

"Okay, guys, I think that's good," Mari said. She placed her mandolin in its black case with green lining that was on the stage beside her.

Eddie stood and walked to the edge of the low stage.

"Mari," Eddie said.

The woman looked up at him. Up close he could see her face clearly and was surprised by her youth compared to the maturity in her music.

"My name's Eddie Holland," he said. "Your Uncle

Domenic asked me to talk to you."

"Oh, right," Mari said. "You just startled me."

"Now I'm concerned that I look like a stalker," Eddie said. "I might need to rethink my wardrobe."

Mari laughed and stepped down off of the stage and shook his hand.

"No, you look good," she said. "I mean, I don't think you look like a stalker. You just surprised me."

After they spoke for a few minutes Eddie and Mari left the club and went to a coffee shop across the street to talk. Eddie ordered a large black coffee and was relieved when the barista didn't insist on calling it a "venti." Mari had an herbal tea.

"So tell me what's been going on," Eddie said.

"It started a few months ago," Mari said. "Seemed innocuous at first, almost sweet actually. I got a note from someone telling me how much they loved my music and how the words really spoke to them. Stuff musicians hear every day."

She sipped her tea as she looked out the front window of the shop at the cars that moved by on 6th Street.

"Then they started coming more often, once a week, then every couple of days," she said. "Then I was getting at least one every day."

"Where did you receive them?" Eddie said.

"At first they all came to Buddy's," she said. "It's my 'home stage' if you will. I play there most often and get shows around town occasionally when I'm not going on mini-tours. Then I'd find them on the windshield of my van. Last week they started coming to my apartment."

"That's not good," Eddie said.

"That's what I thought," she said. "The notes themselves were still positive, until a few days ago. That's when I went to see Uncle Dom."

"Smart move," he said. "He mentioned you have a newer 'break-up' song that didn't go over well with your biggest fan."

"Exactly," Mari said. "The last note was very upsetting. Said I couldn't do that to him, have to give him another chance. Like we actually know each other."

"Do you have the notes with you?" Eddie said.

"No, they're all at home," she said. "I can meet you tomorrow, if you like."

"That would be great," Eddie said. "How about 1:00 here?"

"That works. I'm in here almost every day anyway," She stopped and thought a second. "Do you want to come to the show tonight?"

Eddie liked the idea of seeing a full show.

"That would be great," Eddie said.

"How many and I'll put you on the list?" she said.

"Two," he said. "That's great, I think my girlfriend will love you."

He immediately felt weird and uncomfortable for saying girlfriend to the beautiful young lady.

EDDIE AND EVA got to the club only a few minutes before Mari's set began. Not only were they on the list to bypass the ten-dollar entry fee but also a table in front of the house was reserved for them.

The concert began as they received their drinks, a Shiner Bock for Eddie and a ginger ale for Eva since she was on call for the emergency room. The lights dimmed and Mari walked on stage after her band was in their places.

With the same look back at the drummer and the tapping of her heel he had seen her do in sound check they went into the first song with precision. Mari's voice came in and Eddie glanced around the club to see everyone's attention on her.

CHAPTER 8

The heater was on too high in the room and Eddie tried three times to turn it down with no luck. He checked the hallway but no nurses were to be found.

"It always this hot in here?" Eddie said.

His father sat in his straight back chair looking out the window over the parking lot, hands folded over each other on his lap. Eddie sat back down on the edge of the bed beside him, spending the moments between his one sided conversations by trying to see what his father might be seeing outside.

"So there's this girl," Eddie said. "We've been together for about a year, I guess. She's not like anyone

I've ever met."

Eddie fidgeted on the bed.

"I feel like a twelve year old boy talking about this," Eddie said. "I'm pretty sure I'm going to ask her to move in together. We're rarely apart anyway."

His father had no outward reactions to anything Eddie said. The disease blocked his brain from reaching to the outside world though they told Eddie he hears and understands everything.

A male nurse came in to bring the evening set of pills for his father to take.

"Any way to turn the heat down?" Eddie said.

"I'll check on it," the man said. He put the pills into James Holland's mouth then lifted the small cup of water to his lips and tilted James' head back until he drank the water and swallowed the pills. He put everything back onto the small tray and turned to leave.

"Don't forget about the heat, please," Eddie said.

"Mmm hmm," the man said. The door closed behind him.

"He's not going to check on anything, is he?" Eddie said. He stood and walked over to the shelves and looked at the photographs he'd seen hundreds of times. His sister had arranged them on the shelves when they moved their father into the facility.

A black and white image of his father, young and strong in his Army Ranger fatigues, standing in front of a barrack with a group of other men was always his favorite. He noticed how much he looked now like his father did then and turned to see his dad as he stared out at nothing.

Eddie and his father had always been distant, even before his mother had died. The pressure to join the army and become a Ranger had been constant, and once Eddie told his father he wanted to go to college and pursue working with the FBI, the relationship was more strained than ever.

"You see your own mortality in your father's dying eyes," Eddie said. "Where you've been and more importantly where you'll go. Will I be where you are now in 20 years?"

He turned and sat back on the bed.

"I know you wanted me to sign up, be a Ranger like you," Eddie said. "And I know you never forgave me for not doing it. But I've done my part, Dad. I didn't wear the uniform, but I spent years working with Rangers, SEALS and every other elite team out there. I did more than you know about, than anyone knows about including Gus and Eva. For several years I was more than an analyst. A lot more."

Eddie heard the large cart stop outside the room with the trays of food for the residents who didn't venture out to the common areas for dinner.

"Someday I'll bring Clem to meet you. He's a Ranger, you'd like him. He lost his leg in Afghanistan based on intel my team had a part in getting to him before I even knew him."

Eddie lowered his head.

"That was the beginning of the end for me," Eddie said. "I spent several more years on the job but every time I had to send young men out into the line of fire, I could hardly stand it. I watched men die from thousands of miles away all in the name of defeating an enemy we don't understand."

He looked down at his hands, clean and no callouses.

"It had to be simpler for you. War was war. It was a defined form. You shot at them and they shot at you," Eddie said. "Now it's roadside bombs, drones and children wearing suicide vests into crowded markets."

CHAPTER 9

The Aer Lingus flight landed at JFK airport. Aran Driscoll exited the sky ramp into the terminal and glanced at his watch, which he'd already adjusted to local time. Two hours until the connecting flight to Dallas.

He walked through the people all hurrying to get to their flights or out of the airport and looked at faces and hair until he saw what he needed. A man near his same height but a much heavier build had the same dark hair and light complexion. The man dragged his feet and pulled a rolling suitcase that barely qualified as a carry-on behind him as a woman walked next to him with an equally large build and suitcase.

He followed the couple. They watched gate numbers on the signs over each counter until they arrived at one with the departure sign reading St. Petersburg, Florida. They set the bags down, removed their heavy coats and put them on the seats on either side of them, and collapsed into two of the uncomfortable chairs in the waiting area, leaving an empty seat between them.

Waiting was an art form Aran had perfected back in the IRA. There were times they would sit in the same place for days to watch and take notes on activities of British soldiers and officers. In a public place it is more difficult as you have to look like you aren't out of place. Airports are full of people waiting, but with the added complications of security cameras and police officers everywhere you have to be extra diligent.

An occasional glance at your watch, patting your pocket to make sure you still have your boarding pass, and looking up at the sign at the gate and looking relieved when it still says "on time" look natural. Staring at one person or couple for extended periods of time does not look normal and can draw unwanted attention, especially if there is reason for security tapes to be reviewed later.

Aran leaned on the wall across the hall from the couple and waited. It was 40 minutes until the plane to

St. Petersburg departed, which meant ten to 15 minutes before boarding began. Right on cue with minutes to go before boarding, the large man stood and shuffled his feet back across the hall and into the men's room and Aran followed him.

No less than a dozen men were in the restroom, which gave Aran easy opportunity to complete his task. Within moments in the cramped space he was able to brush past the man, his own right hand tapping the man's shoulder as he squeezed past him and said "excuse me" with an American accent. His left hand lifted the wallet out of the man's jeans and dropped it into the large custom sewn pocket inside his own jacket.

Out of the bathroom he turned left and was ten gates away before the man was washing his hands after using the bathroom. He pulled the wallet out and opened it. The brown leather was worn and had a curve to it from being trapped beneath the large man for too many years. Aran glanced at the driver's license then pulled out the bank debit card. There were two one hundred dollar bills that he pulled and tucked into his shirt pocket. He stopped at the next ATM and reached up with his left hand to casually lean on the machine while covering the camera with his palm before he inserted the card. At the prompt for a PIN he entered the birthday and month off of the driver's license from the man's wallet, 0621, and heard a beep that the number was incorrect. He tried again with the birth year, 1974. The screen changed and asked him if he would like to make a withdrawal.

The disposable phone he'd used once before the flight was at the bottom of a trashcan at Shannon Airport. He stepped into an identical convenience shop at JFK airport and used some of the cash he'd just taken out of the ATM and bought a new phone.

After locating his gate he sat to wait for his flight and opened the new phone, turned it on, and texted a blank message to the same number he had in Shannon. He turned the phone off and put it in his bag.

The wallet he'd stolen was back in the bathroom where he'd lifted it, on the floor under the sink, ready to be found and taken by someone else or turned in to airport security.

CHAPTER 10

E ddie parked on 6th Street outside the coffee shop and found Mari Simon already camped out on a sofa with a small table in the window, scribbling notes into a yellow legal pad.

"Can I have your autograph?" Eddie said as he walked up to her.

Mari looked up and pulled the ear buds out that were hidden under her long hair.

"Oh, hey, Eddie," she said. "What did you say?"

"Nothing," Eddie sat down on a wooden chair across from her. "Just said hi. Working on a new song?"

"Always," she said. "You write 20 to hopefully get one

you keep. Sometimes you take part of several to make one song."

"Is it hard for you, writing?" Eddie said.

"Sometimes, but you usually work ideas around in your head before writing them down then they flow out," Mari said. "Some of the most famous songs were written in minutes."

"So there's no mystical power at work?" Eddie said.

She shook her head and turned her nose up at the idea.

"I heard this singer-songwriter type guy in concert once, maybe 30 people in the audience who were all there for the act following him," Mari said. "Before singing a new song he said 'when this song first presented itself to me to write' and I almost choked on my beer I laughed so hard. People were staring at me."

"That's pretty pretentious," Eddie said. "What do you do with the ones you don't keep?"

"They're all packed in boxes and stuffed in notebooks," Mari said. "Sometimes a month or a year later you'll think of one of the old songs and figure out what was missing from it, so they never get thrown away."

"Guess that's how they keep finding new songs by long dead singers," Eddie said.

"Probably," Mari said then patted the cushion beside her. "You're too far away."

The large table separating them put them more than six feet away from each other.

"I'd rather not yell. Come over here."

Eddie hesitated for a moment then stood and joined Mari on her sofa and left a couple of feet between them. She picked a shoebox up off of the floor and sat it in the empty space he had left.

"Here they are," she said.

"Wow, that's a lot more than I expected," Eddie said. "How long has this been going on?"

"A few months now," she said. "Once they started coming every day they really stacked up."

"It's good you thought to save them," he said.

"At first I thought they might give me some inspiration for a new song, then after a while I had more of a feeling that they might just be evidence at some point," she said.

Eddie pulled the stack of envelopes out and began from the bottom of the stack, the earliest ones, and read each one until he got to the latest disturbing note.

"There's definitely a progression," he said. "Even in the early ones, each note or every few notes gets a little more personal as the attachment grows stronger."

"What does that mean?" Mari said.

"Means this guy is pretty hooked," Eddie said. "In his mind you two were in a full on relationship. Looks like he's seen a lot of your shows. Do you have a calendar showing all the nights you played?"

"Sure," Mari said.

She flipped to the back of her notebook to lists of dates, club names and cities with her own personal notes on the show and how she felt it had gone and her set list. "I had one tour of Texas, Oklahoma and Kansas a month or so ago, other than that they're all over at Buddy's or a couple other places in town. Also had one private show, a wedding."

Eddie took the notebook and flipped through the envelopes, comparing show dates to the postmarks and put small checkmarks beside each item in the notebook that he felt lined up with a note.

"In a lot of the notes he references a show the night before, or even that night," Eddie said. "He may even have written some while at a show."

He finished reviewing all of the dates.

"He's a busy guy," Eddie said. "Almost all of the dates in his notes line up with your shows, including Houston, Dallas, Tulsa and Kansas City."

"Really?" Mari said.

"That includes the wedding reception six weeks ago," Eddie said.

"How?" Mari said. "It was a private party."

"It's pretty easy to crash a wedding," Eddie said. "Especially a large one. Everyone assumes you're a friend of the other wedding party. Avoid being in front of the bride and groom at the same time and you have free booze and food and a dance floor full of inebriated guests."

"That's crazy," Mari said. "I could never do that."

"You mind if I take the letters with me?" Eddie said. "I'd like to try to lift a fingerprint."

"Sure, anything you need," Mari said.

Eddie drank his coffee and leaned back on the sofa as Mari nursed her tea. They sat without talking for longer than Eddie found comfortable.

"So that was your girlfriend you brought to the show last night? She's beautiful," Mari broke the silence.

"Oh, thanks," Eddie said. "I can't take any credit for that. I'm just happy she likes to be with me."

"Come on, why wouldn't she," Mari said. "You're quite a catch."

Eddie was now more uncomfortable than he was when they were silent.

"You two pretty serious?" Mari said.

"I am. Can't speak for her," Eddie changed the subject back to the stalker. "Are these all of the notes?"

"Oh, yeah, just got one this morning," Mari grabbed a folded piece of paper from her backpack and handed it to him. "Wasn't as mean, but definitely didn't give me a warm and fuzzy feeling either."

Eddie read to himself.

> *You broke my heart but I will go on.*
> *I know we can be happy together.*
> *I know you will love me (again).*
> *I miss you and I miss your smell.*

"He said he misses your smell."

"Yeah, creepy, huh," Mari said.

"That means he's been close enough, well, to smell you," Eddie said. He considered making a Hannibal Lector reference but decided that might be even creepier than the note.

"Can you smell me?" Mari said.

Eddie looked up at her from the note. Her eyes were on him, waiting on an answer.

"No," he lied.

She leaned over the box of notes towards him.

"How about now," she said. Her face turned and her

cheek was inches from his face.

She ran her hand through her hair and it touched the tip of his nose then fell back to her shoulder. Lilacs, he thought to himself. Her eyes were locked on his even when he wasn't looking at her, which he was trying not to do.

"Yeah," Eddie said. "It's kinda flowery."

"Typical guy," Mari leaned back in her seat and reached for her cup of tea. "Flowery, indeed. French lilac."

"That was my second guess," Eddie said.

She drank her tea and he enjoyed the brief silence, spending the moments contemplating whether she was flirting with him, hitting on him, or just being herself and he was reading it all wrong. He decided, and hoped, it was the latter.

CHAPTER 11

On the ground at Dallas Fort Worth Airport, Aran Driscoll followed his same game plan from New York and within a few minutes of having landed and cleared customs with a counterfeit passport he had the wallet of a man who minutes later was boarding a flight to Portland, Oregon. Aran looked through the wallet on the way to the car rental booth and found an Oregon driver's license, six hundred dollars in cash, an American Express card and a couple of Visa cards.

"Do you have a reservation, sir?"

"Sure don't," Aran said with no trace of his Irish accent. "I'm visiting my sister and she was supposed to pick me up but she wasn't able to last minute, something about one of the kids getting sick at school."

"I understand," the clerk looked at the driver's license he'd provided from the freshly stolen wallet. "Mr. Sutherland?"

"Ahh, yes, the photograph," Aran said. "I lost a lot of weight over the last year. Weight Watchers."

"Good for you, sir," she said. "Would you like a full size car today?"

"What do you have in an SUV?" Aran said.

Aran left the rental agency in a grey Chevy Suburban with a full tank of gas. He estimated the flight time from Dallas to Portland was three hours. Before the real Mr. Sutherland landed in Oregon and began cancelling his credit cards he planned to have the large SUV well behind him.

He pulled to the side of the highway and opened the disposable phone he'd bought in New York and turned it on. A single text message came in that said only "Hillsboro." He looked at the map the rental clerk had given him and traced the route from Dallas south and found the town of Hillsboro. Looking at the distance to travel then at his watch he texted back "2 hours" and pulled onto the highway.

He'd worked with his handler for more than a decade

and they had a system that worked well for them. Minimal information passed back and forth and generally only just before it was needed. The person on the other end of the phone had learned Aran's needs and could predict what he would want and need at any certain location. The two had never spoken on the phone or met in person, but Aran relied on and trusted his handler like no one else he had ever known.

With the personal nature of this mission Aran was more involved in the planning. His handler had used an asset in Alabama to blackmail a young army corporal into stealing guns and explosive ordnance from Redstone Arsenal outside Huntsville. As Aran drove from Dallas to Hillsboro, Corporal Hector Castellano was making the final drive across several states with a U-Haul filled with everything Aran needed to go after Eddie Holland.

Aran arrived in Hillsboro an hour later, stopped at an auto parts store and bought some tools then drove around the town until he found a deserted retail building and pulled in behind and parked. He took the tools out, slid over to the passenger seat and began to take the dashboard apart.

Two hours after sending his last text message he was parked on an empty farm road west of Hillsboro and sent another message with directions to his location. It took two minutes to get the reply: "five minutes."

Aran closed the phone and put it in his leather bag then leaned down and reached under the dash.

The U-Haul truck pulled onto the farm road and stopped a few car lengths from the grey SUV. Aran got out with his bag and closed the door and walked towards the truck. A young Latino man with a tight green polo shirt got out of the truck and walked towards him. Aran could see the tail of the shirt unnaturally stretched around the man's right side.

"Hector?" Aran said.

"Yes," Hector Castellano said.

"You have everything you were told to get?" Aran said, not hiding his true voice.

"Yes sir, I do," Hector said. "What about my mother? Do you have her?"

"No," Aran said. "We'll be in touch on where you can pick her up. Keys are in the ignition."

Aran began to walk past the man towards the U-Haul and saw movement from the corner of his eye. He dropped his bag and turned on his heel as his left arm came up to block the soldier's pistol as it was pulled from the holster under the green polo and raised to aim at his head. In the same motion he moved into Hector's body, landing his right elbow square in the young man's face. His arm continued around as Aran turned his back on the soldier then brought his left elbow back into the ribs, cracking two. As Hector fell to the ground Aran took the soldier's huge Smith & Wesson .45 pistol and flipped the safety switch on as he shoved the barrel into the back of his jeans.

"Did you think you were gonna be a hero today?" Aran said. "Next time you try to hide a cannon, don't wear a tight shirt. I knew you had a gun the second you got out of the truck."

Hector had his face to the dirt, sucking in air to recover from the strike to his face and the cracked ribs.

"I just want my mother back," Hector said.

"As far as I know she's at feckin' bingo right now," Aran said. "Now get in that truck and drive home, little soldier boy."

Aran walked away and climbed into the U-Haul, pulled the .45 from his jeans and put it on the seat beside him. The shifter in reverse, he backed up until he could turn the truck around on the gravel road.

He saw Hector stand as he pulled away, his lips moving as he was likely swearing at Aran. As the man went out of view, Aran timed out the actions behind him in his head. Hector would walk to the SUV and climb in, maybe look at his bloodied face in the mirror, then he'd notice the torn up dashboard and probably call Aran some more names.

Then Hector would turn the key, which would send a signal to the vehicle's computer to turn the starter and engage the engine. As soon as the first spark plug received its blast of electricity, the explosives lined shock tube Aran had removed from the airbag and attached to the spark plug would ignite and send a charge to the fuel line a foot away. The fuel inside the rubber tubing would begin to burn as it travelled towards the back of the truck. The flame would reach the three-quarter full fuel tank and ignite the vapors that rested above the gasoline.

From his rearview mirror, Aran watched the Chevy Suburban lift off of the ground, surrounded by bright flames after the burning vapors had heated up enough and caused the liquid fuel to explode. He rolled the U-Haul window down and tossed the Smith & Wesson to the side of the road and kept driving.

He kept the speed of the truck under the limit by five miles per hour and turned the radio on and tuned it to a news radio station. It was five minutes before he saw the first police car racing to the scene of the burning SUV. A few minutes later he was on the interstate headed south.

The U-Haul crossed the city line into Austin at

midnight. He parked the large truck on the street outside a self-storage business where it wouldn't seem out of place then walked two blocks and took a cab from a convenience store parking lot to the university campus. A short time later he left campus in an older BMW with Texas plates, the heater turned on full blast to compensate for the cold air coming in from the shattered passenger side window.

He made his way through the city to an address that had come through in a text message during his drive in the U-Haul.

CHAPTER 12

The restaurant was loud, but Eddie had thought ahead and reserved the small private room in the back where they could talk at a normal volume and still hear each other. It had been a year since his first date with Eva.

"So, Eva," Shelley said. "Why are we just now meeting?"

Eva turned and looked at Eddie who pretended not to hear what had been asked.

"I think we can thank the man of many secrets over here."

"Oh, he may have his secrets about what he does but I

can tell you anything you want to know about him when he was growing up," Shelley said.

"And right there is why I waited so long to do this," Eddie said.

He and Eva sat together on one side of the table facing his sister Shelley and her husband Samuel. His relationship with his brother-in-law was strained at best.

"Eddie, have you been working lately?" Samuel threw a passive aggressive question towards him that went unnoticed by his wife.

"When I want to," Eddie said. "Right now I have a private job that Shelley sent my way."

"You're still using Eddie at the law firm?" Samuel interrupted his wife's conversation with Eva mid sentence. "I thought we talked about that."

Eddie's sister and her family had been taken into protective custody at a safe house outside of Austin for a week due to a case that he had worked for Shelley's law firm. After that, Samuel told his wife to never have him hired again.

"This is for Father Domenic, not work," Shelley said. She directed herself towards her brother. "Can you tell us anything about it?"

Eddie hesitated.

"I'd really rather not talk about it," he said. "I'm still

working through all of the details."

"So do you have any leads at least?" Shelley said.

"I'm working on some things," Eddie said.

"I feel like I'm watching one of those police briefings where they talk and talk and don't say anything at all," Shelley said.

"You should be used to that working with lawyers all day," Eddie said.

A new bottle of wine came that Eddie had selected, a Malbec from Argentina. Fresh glasses were poured for both couples.

"So Eva," Shelley said. "Do you plan on going into private practice?"

"Eventually, but right now I'm really enjoying emergency medicine," Eva said. "I figure I have another couple of years that I can handle the long hours and pretty much always being on call before I burn out."

"Do you want kids?" Shelley said.

"Whoa!" Eddie said and threw his white napkin into the middle of the table. "Flag on the play!"

"What! It's a fair question," Shelley said. "I didn't say 'Do you want kids with my baby brother.' I just wondered if she wants kids at some point."

"It's okay, Eddie," Eva said. "I don't mind."

Eva took a long drink of her wine.

"Yes, I do," Eva said. "I'm the oldest of three girls, the closest being eight years younger than me so I really helped raise them."

"I understand," Shelley said. "Eddie's the baby, so he was never around little kids much as we grew up. But being a few years older than him and would dress him up in my old clothes."

"Oh, really?" Eva said. She looked at Eddie who was staring into his wine and wishing he were somewhere else right then.

"How did he look in a dress?"

"Adorable," Shelley said.

Eddie rode in the passenger seat of Eva's Fiat 500 as they drove back to her house. He knew he would probably have at least a glass of wine too many, if not a bottle, and planned ahead for Eva to drive.

"I am so sorry about that," Eddie said.

"What, your sister's questions?" Eva said. "That was just a big sister watching out for her little brother. I'm so much harder on my sisters when I meet their boyfriends."

"Still, I'm sorry, and I'm sorry in advance for every other time she asks you things like that," he said. "So what about your family, when do I have to meet them?"

"*Have* to meet them?" she said.

"You know what I mean," Eddie said.

"Oh, I know what you mean," Eva said. "And soon enough."

They rode in silence as Eva seemed like she was looking for the best way to ask Eddie a question. Eddie glanced over at her then back out the passenger window.

"You're wondering about my father," Eddie said.

"How the hell did you know that?" Eva said.

"It's my job to read people," Eddie said. "Plus it's logical. You met my only sibling today. You know my mother died when I was a kid, and I never talk about my Dad."

"Right. Logical," Eva said.

"Don't you need some time to recover from meeting Shelley and her wonderful husband?"

"He's not that bad," Eva said.

"Yes, he is," Eddie said.

"What's with you two? Why don't you get along?"

"He's resented me working for the FBI since he and Shelley met. I think he's always felt he was competing with me for some reason," Eddie said. "Then my nephew begins to emulate me. He started Tae Kwon Do, and is a natural. His father has no athletic ability. Then he started reading everything he could find about the FBI from his school library."

"And I'm sure you threw no fuel on the fire?"

"Of course not. I just gave him a patch from my first Gi and got him a private tour of the Hoover Building when they visited D.C. a few years ago."

"Subtle," Eva said.

CHAPTER 13

T he diner was empty except for an old man sitting at the counter sipping from a coffee cup like it was good whiskey. Eddie and Gus sat in their usual booth in the window, their plates empty of the food that had been on them.

"Adrian Pierce got arraigned today. He's 17, but they charged him as an adult," Gus said.

"Who is Adrian Pierce?" Eddie said.

"The shooter from the school," Gus said. "Jesus, you don't know the name of the kid you kept from killing a bunch of children?"

"Unnecessary information," Eddie said. "If he was on

the loose and we were trying to bring him in, I'd be concerned with who he is. But he's locked up in a four by four and won't see the light of day again."

"The cells at county are actually six by nine," Gus said.

"What luxury," Eddie said.

"How did you know he wouldn't shoot you?" Gus said.

"What?" Eddie said.

"Adrian Pierce. You charged him with a shotgun aimed at you. How did you know he wouldn't shoot you?"

"I didn't know," Eddie said. "But I figured the principal was an adrenaline kill. The kid had gone to the school all pumped up and ready and the principal confronted him and he released all that energy and rage. After that he was in panic mode. He might have killed someone else, but I don't think he really wanted to."

"But you said he deliberately raised the shotgun to shoot you," Gus said.

"He did," Eddie said. "The way he handled the shotgun, I could tell he wasn't a shooter. He wasn't comfortable with it. I knew I had time to get to him, that he'd hesitate on the trigger."

"And if you hadn't gotten to him in time?" Gus said.

"Then you'd be sitting here talking to yourself."

"Think he was opting for suicide-by-cop?" Gus said.

"I do, and I wasn't going to let that happen," Eddie said.

"That why you tackled him instead of following our training to take him down?" Gus said.

"Like you said, he's 17. He's a kid," Eddie said. "He has his whole life in front of him. Unfortunately it'll be a life lived in prison, but at least he gets the opportunity to be punished for what he did. He'll be lucky not to get the chair."

"Texas uses lethal injection," Gus said.

"See? Kids today have it too easy," Eddie said.

The two men took sips of the hot coffee.

"He ever say why he did it?" Eddie said.

"Yeah. He said he was trying to prove he was 'ready for battle'," Gus said.

"With who?" Eddie said. "What battle?"

"No idea," Gus said.

Conversation paused as Eddie filled both of their cups with coffee from the carafe the waitress had left for them. Gus put in half a pouch of sugar, stirred, and lifted the cup to take a sip.

Eddie finished filling his cup and reached to set the carafe down at the end of the table. As his hand pulled away the mug in front of him shattered. Pieces of ceramic flew into both men's chests and faces. They looked at the broken mug and the scarring on the table then up to the plate glass window. A single small round hole was just above their eye level.

Another bullet came through the glass and hit the carafe in front of Eddie and hot coffee exploded into the air. Eddie and Gus both lunged out of the booth and moved along the floor to get behind the counter.

"Everybody get down!" Gus yelled. "Get behind the counter!"

The old man in the corner looked up from his newspaper at the two men crawling on the floor and the waitresses diving for the relative safety behind the counter. The man put his coffee cup down, stood, and walked over to the counter and sat down on the floor behind it.

Gus had his phone out giving the address to the local police department.

"Shots fired," Gus said. "We need units here immediately."

They continued hiding behind the counter. Eddie and Gus took turns looking up over the edge to try to spot the shooter. It was two minutes before the first police car pulled up with lights on and siren blaring, then another half dozen came in over the following minutes.

"We need a perimeter set up and eyes out to make sure the shooter is gone," Gus was on the phone with the officer in charge outside the diner.

The large black van from the SWAT department skidded to a stop on the street and ten armed men jumped out of the back, assault weapons raised and pointed away from the building as each hit the ground and ran to secure the area. Two of the officers came to the door and one at a time they escorted the waitress, cook and the old man out of the diner and into the backroom while the rest of the officers cleared the building.

Eddie and Gus stood and remained in the seating area of the diner and walked to the booth where they'd been sitting.

"Long gone by now," Eddie looked out the window and scanned the buildings and cars down the road.

"Incredible shot," Gus said. "If that's what he was aiming for."

"Shitty shot if it wasn't," Eddie said.

Gus stepped up onto the bench seat of the booth to the plate glass window. The holes in the glass were no more than a third of an inch around. He put his head at eye level to the holes and turned to look to where the carafe had been.

"He had a down angle," Gus said. He turned and looked back out the window to the distant buildings.

"Not many tall buildings down that way," Eddie said. "There's the Belvedere Hotel, but that's, what, eight blocks away?"

"I'll get a team in here to check the angle to get a good read on where the shooter was," Gus said.

Eddie went to the end of the table and squatted and peered from table height up to the hole in the glass.

"Or we just head to the Belvedere," he said. "It's the only option for this shot."

"I'll talk to the locals, get them to send a some uniforms down with us," Gus said. "We may have to clear a few rooms."

The men drove the eight blocks down to the five-story hotel, moving slowly down the road as they scanned the sidewalks.

"Snipers love to see the aftermath of their work," Eddie said. "Keep an eye out."

They pulled into the circle drive used for unloading guest luggage and left the car and went into the lobby. The hotel had changed owners years ago and had turned into a something just slightly above a flophouse. Guests ranged from recent parolees from the county jail to alcoholics and cheaters kicked out of their homes by their spouses.

"This place could use a little updating," Eddie said.

"More than a little," Gus said. "Hasn't changed in years."

"You been here before?" Eddie said.

"High school, when it was still a hotel," Gus said. "I brought Janine Clement here on prom night. I thought I was hot shit."

"Did she?" Eddie said.

"No," Gus said. "She called me cheap and left. Heard later she'd ended up with Mike Lange. Lost her virginity in the back seat of his mother's minivan."

"And she thought you were cheap?" Eddie said.

At the front desk a Latina lady in a white tee shirt and jeans turned from her chair behind the counter, a television blaring a Spanish language soap opera.

"Help you?" she said.

Gus flashed his badge. "We need access to all west facing rooms, starting from the top floor and going down."

"Got a warrant?" she said.

"Got a green card?" Gus said.

"I was born in Amarillo, asshole," she said.

"How about the rest of your staff?" Gus said.

She hesitated then grabbed a key from under the

counter and handed it to him.

"Anyone staying in those rooms?" Eddie said.

"Nobody wants the rooms on the west side," she said. "The air doesn't work and those rooms are ovens from noon on. Hell, I never go in if I don't have to."

"No air conditioning in Austin?" Eddie said. "That's inhumane."

"Says the man with no air conditioning in his car," Gus said.

"It's a convertible," Eddie said.

"You never put the top down."

"I don't like to mess up my hair," Eddie said.

Six uniformed officers walked through the front door of the hotel. A man who had been sleeping on a sofa in the far corner of the lobby got up and walked out the front door, keeping his head turned away from the policemen. Gus turned back to the woman.

"We're going to need more keys," he said.

She reached back under the counter and pulled two more keys and handed them over.

"Don't make a mess in there," she said.

"Right," Eddie said. "Maid's day off?"

Gus handed the keys to the officers and gave them instructions. Gus and Eddie were going to start on the fifth floor, a pair of officers on the fourth and a pair on the third while the remaining two began to question people in the hotel and canvassing the neighborhood. They walked to the elevator and Eddie pressed the button.

"It don't work," the woman said from her chair behind the counter.

"Of course it doesn't," Eddie said. The men turned and began to climb the steps to the right of the elevator.

Eddie and Gus got to the top floor and began from one end of the hallway to work through the six rooms with west facing views. The first three rooms were undisturbed, down to the layer of dust on the flat surfaces.

As Gus put the key into the door of the fourth room he paused.

"This doorknob has been used today," Gus said. "The others were all dusty. This one isn't."

Gus pulled his Sig Sauer pistol from its holster and turned the key with his left hand, careful not to touch the handle and disturb any fingerprints. He glanced back at Eddie and nodded a three count then pushed the door open, the weapon raised to eye level scanning the room from right to left as he took three quick steps in.

Eddie followed, unarmed, and turned to the left to check behind the wall to the kitchenette.

"Clear," Gus said.

"Clear," Eddie said.

Gus stepped to the window and looked along the bottom edge.

"The window's been opened," Gus said. "It's still unlocked and there's some scuff marks in the paint."

He turned to the bed and knelt down.

"Depression marks on the bed. Shooter sat here, rifle braced on the window ledge," he turned and looked down the street. "I can't even read the name of the diner from here."

Gus pulled out his phone and dialed the number for the police chief.

"We found where the shooter was," Gus said. "Would you send the crime scene team in?" They spoke another minute then hung up.

Eddie stared out the window.

"Whoever it was is a pro," Eddie said.

"Think they were after one of us?" Gus said.

"Either that or he really hates coffee," Eddie said.

CHAPTER 14

E ddie stood in the back of the club and watched Mari perform for the second night in a row and began to feel like a stalker himself. He drank slowly from a bottle of Shiner Bock and scanned the crowd.

Mari always pulled a decent audience, even on weeknights. Her appeal with the locals as well as with the college students insured Buddy kept booking her whenever she'd play. She wasn't getting rich off of the shows but it was paying her rent and her parents still sent her money every month.

The audience was respectful of the music and hardly anybody spoke during the songs. Eddie saw mostly groups of two or more people. He looked at the tables with couples and tried to figure out how long each had been dating by their body language. One couple was obviously married, he thought. Their attention drawn to the music and the performance more than to each other with a comfort between them that only comes from years of being together.

To their left was the opposite end of the spectrum. A first or second date as the young man paid far more attention to his date than he did to Mari Simon, which was a difficult task. Eddie wondered for a moment how he and Eva would look to a casual bystander.

There were very few people standing or sitting alone. One man caught his eye at a table a few rows back from the stage and off to the side. His attention stayed on Mari but a few times he made notes in a small spiral notebook he would take out of his coat pocket hanging on the back of his chair and replace after writing.

Mari played her final song of the night and thanked the audience and followed her band off of the stage. The crowd slowly dispersed, most having already settled their tabs. Eddie watched the man as he pulled his coat on then walked out the front door of the club and Eddie followed him.

Stepping onto the sidewalk he looked right then left

and didn't see the man. Eddie went to the intersection on his left and looked down the side street with no luck and went back into the bar and found Buddy.

"There was a man sitting by himself there," Eddie said and pointed to the table in the now empty club. "Do you know if he ran a tab?"

"Let me check," Buddy motioned to the waitress that had worked the floor and she came over to the bar where the two men stood. He asked her about the man.

"Sure did," she said as she pulled all of her night's receipts out of the pocket in her apron tied around her waist and flipped through them. "Here it is, table 16."

Eddie took the receipt from the waitress and looked it over. He'd had two beers, nachos and had given a two-dollar tip.

"Big spender," Eddie said.

"Most of our people tip well, but you get the occasional cheapskate," the waitress said.

Looking at the bottom of the receipt was an unreadable signature, but the name was printed by the cash register just above the scribbling.

"Jacob Lee," Eddie said. "Thanks, I appreciate it." He handed the waitress a ten-dollar bill and she smiled and thanked him and walked away.

"Is this about Mari's stalker?" Buddy said.

"Yup," Eddie said.

"Got any leads?" Buddy asked.

"I do now," Eddie said.

Mari ran from behind the stage out of breath.

"Eddie, thank god you're here," she said.

"What's up?" Eddie said.

"This was under my windshield wiper," Mari handed him a piece of paper that had been folded.

'GET RID OF HIM' was written in large red letters taking up an entire side of the paper.

"I'm guessing it means you?" Mari said.

"If so then it means he was here last night and tonight," Eddie said. "And maybe even saw us at the coffee shop together. Buddy, any way to go through receipts and see if that same guy was here last night?"

"Sure," Buddy said. "But it'll take a while. I can call you tomorrow."

Eddie left the bar and walked two blocks to his car then drove home to his apartment. He parked his Karmann Ghia across the street from his building, two cars behind the dark green BMW where Aran Driscoll waited.

CHAPTER 15

Morning came and Eddie was up and getting ready for a cool air run when his cellphone rang. Not recognizing the number, he left the phone and pulled the door to his apartment closed behind him. It was more than an hour later when he returned. He saw the red light blinking on the phone as he passed and picked it up to check the voicemail.

"Mr. Holland," a thick Irish brogue came through the earpiece. "We've never met, but we will. I hope you enjoyed your coffee yesterday. That was just a little preview, a tease. I look forward to killing you soon."

Eddie looked at the phone, the words of the message

running through his head. He copied the phone number and sent a text to Gus with the number and a note, "need a lookup on this number."

He took a long shower then dressed and pulled on his straw duckbill cap. He left the apartment and jogged down the steps from his apartment then along the sidewalk towards his car parked across the street. His phone beeped and he stopped to read the message from Gus.

"Burner phone activated yesterday in Dallas. Should I be worried?"

Eddie contemplated a response but put the phone back in his pocket without sending one. He walked to his car and got in, put his left foot on the clutch and turned the key in the ignition and nothing happened. No click, no engine starting. He got out of the car, left the door open and walked back across the street and pulled his phone out and sent a reply to Gus.

'Send EOD to my apartment now.'

Eddie sat on the step to watch his car from a distance. Ten minutes later two large trucks pulled up.

Sergeant Buckholtz had been with the regional Explosive Ordnance Disposal squad for fourteen years and now stood in front of Eddie Holland, across the street from his old Volkswagen convertible.

"So the car didn't start?" Sergeant Buckholtz said.

"Right," Eddie said.

"Did you think about calling AAA instead of the bomb squad?"

The two large trucks blocked the road fifty feet on either side of Eddie's car and a half dozen police cars were setting up a perimeter.

"You don't get it," Eddie said. "It always starts. I've had the car since I was 16. It's as dependable as a German watch."

"You mean Swiss watch?" Buckholtz said.

"No, it's a German — never mind," Eddie said. "It just always starts."

"Don't you think the starter might have gone out?" Sergeant Buckholtz said.

"No, I don't," Eddie said.

Gus arrived and walked up to the two men and showed his credentials to the sergeant.

"So what's going on?" Gus said.

"My car didn't start," Eddie said.

Gus looked across the street at the light red and rust colored car Eddie had driven since high school.

"But your car always starts," Gus said.

"That's what I've been trying to tell the Sergeant,"

"You think this is related to the diner?" Gus said.

"I do," Eddie said.

Gus turned to the short but wide explosives specialist.

"Sergeant, we have a high probability of an explosive device in this car," Gus said.

"Seriously?" Sergeant Buckholtz said.

"Seriously," Gus said.

The Sergeant turned and began barking orders to the team of men and women waiting by their trucks. Several of the technicians began pulling on the heavy bomb proof suits and helmets while others pulled the remote controlled robot out and sent it to begin searching and scanning the car.

Eddie and Gus watched from the sidewalk.

"I hope you have something," Gus said. "So what are you thinking?"

"The phone number you traced was from a voicemail," Eddie said. "Some guy asking how my coffee was yesterday and that he was looking forward to killing me."

"So if your starter isn't actually out, then this is likely connected," Gus said.

"Correct," Eddie said. "But it could be the starter."

Gus turned and looked at Eddie as he shook his head then back to the scene across the street.

The robot reached its arms under the car with

cameras and sensors while the Sergeant and several others watched on large LCD screens in the back of the truck. Then the robot pulled away from the car and rolled back to its operator. The two men watched Sergeant Buckholtz make the walk back over to them.

"There's a device attached below the fuel tank at the front of the car and several blocks of C4," Buckholtz said. "We were able to remove the connection from the detonator to the explosives."

"So you can take the bomb out now?" Eddie said.

"No," Buckholtz almost appeared to be smiling. "We'll be transporting the vehicle to a safe location and will conduct further tests for evidence. Then we will be detonating the explosives with our own ordnance to ensure no hazardous materials are left. It's the safest way to do so."

"Detonate?" Eddie said. "You're going to blow my car up?"

"Yes, sir," Buckholtz said. "You might want to start looking for a new car."

Buckholtz walked off and over the next half hour the old VW was prepared then rolled onto a flat bed truck, covered with a thick blast resistant tarp, then driven away.

"Wow," Gus said.

"Yeah, wow," Eddie said.

"I thought it was going to outlive both of us," Gus said.

"It would have," Eddie said.

"So who wants you dead this time?" Gus said.

"Some Irish asshole," Eddie said.

"Narrows it down a little," Gus said.

"A little," Eddie said.

They watched as the EOD team packed up their gear and left.

"Need a ride?" Gus said.

"Looks that way," Eddie said.

CHAPTER 16

Eddie sat in Gus's office at the FBI satellite field office. They drank coffee and between guesses about who might have wanted to kill Eddie, who ranged from ex-girlfriends to the Illuminati, and recalled moments with the Karmann Ghia as if the car had been a friend.

"We sent your phone up to Dallas to the Regional Computer Forensics Lab for better analysis," Gus said. "We can only do so much here, or even at the field office in San Antonio. Here's a new phone, same number."

Gus slid a phone across the table to Eddie.

"Not much they can do," Eddie said. "It was an

incoming call."

"I know, but it's all we have physically, aside from, well," Gus paused.

"The remains of the only car I've ever owned," Eddie said.

"Yeah, that," Gus said. "Meanwhile we're tracking any info we can on the incoming call. It's more difficult since it was a voicemail. They'll analyze the voice to match against any known baddies."

"Hope it helps," Eddie said.

"And we're waiting on a warrant to get any other traffic from that number," Gus said.

"Won't be much, if any," Eddie said. "Not if the guy is a pro."

"Which he likely is," Gus said. "You have any ops back in your DC days that targeted an Irish national?"

"Not that I remember," Eddie said. "I was counter terrorism with a joint task force full of CIA guys. So most of my targets were middle eastern since that's all the Agency thinks can be terrorists."

"Well, keep thinking about it, see if anything comes to mind," Gus said. "Maybe call someone from your old squad."

"I already have a message in with my boss from the task force," Eddie said. "But he's a desk jockey now putting in his last couple years until retirement at the Hoover building."

They drank their coffee.

"Any luck tracing the explosives from my car?" Eddie said.

"C4, nothing wild," Gus said. "But EOD packed up what they could and shipped it to Quantico."

"Why place explosives and not wire them to blow with the turn of the key?" Eddie said.

"What do you mean?" Gus said.

"He clearly disabled the ignition even though he wired the bomb," Eddie said. "He had to know I'd find the C4."

"Maybe he wants to screw with you," Gus said. "Or maybe he wants to hurt you before getting to the main act."

"It worked," Eddie said. "I have a rental Impala now. That hurts."

"What, don't enjoy feeling like you're driving a Bureau car?" Gus said.

"The car is fine, it just isn't my car," Eddie said. "It's too… comfortable."

"Yeah, must really be annoying having working heat and air conditioning," Gus said.

"Dammit," Eddie said. "All my CD's were in there.

Think I could get them back? Have they destroyed the car yet?"

"You owned a dozen CD's and half of them were Lyle Lovett," Gus said. "I think you can replace your collection pretty easily."

Eddie's phone rang on Gus's desk and he answered, spoke for a minute, and then hung up.

"What was that?" Gus said.

"My stalker case," Eddie said. "Buddy found receipts from the same guy from five other nights that Mari Simon was playing."

"Maybe just a fan?" Gus said.

"Or maybe too big a fan," Eddie said. "I'm gonna go check this out. Let me know if you hear anything."

CHAPTER 17

After stopping at the workstation set aside for him at the FBI office for a few minutes, Eddie was in his rented tan Chevy Impala following directions from the voice on his phone to the home of Jacob Lee. He drove south from the office, through the university and then east away from downtown. He stopped in front of a two-story apartment building that had seen its best days decades earlier.

"You have arrived," the voice from his phone's GPS said.

"Not in the way I'd always hoped," Eddie said. He shut off the navigation on the phone and slid it into his pocket as he got out of the car.

On his third and loudest series of knocks he heard activity inside apartment 113. Out of habit he stepped to his right to be out of the way of the peephole or stray bullets. From the looks of the building and the neighborhood the bullets could come from any direction.

"Who is it?" a voice yelled from the other side of the door.

"Eddie Holland."

"Who the hell is Eddie Holland?"

"Me," Eddie said.

"Smart ass," the voice said. "You a cop?"

"No," Eddie said. "I'm a private investigator."

"What do you want?"

"I'd like to talk with you about your presence at Buddy's Music Saloon on several different occasions."

Eddie heard the deadbolt slide then the doorknob turned and the door opened. Facing him through the door was a short man in his forties who looked like he was in his fifties and dressed like he was in his twenties. The smell of alcohol and stale marijuana smoke coming from the apartment hit Eddie in the face.

"You wanna come in?" Jacob Lee said.

Eddie looked through the open door and turned his

head again at the smell.

"No, I really don't, Mr. Lee," Eddie said. "Would you mind coming outside?"

"Whatever. Guess I could use a little fresh air," Jacob said. "Gimme a minute."

The door closed and stayed that way for several minutes. Then Jacob Lee came out, dressed as he had been but with a cheap box store fedora on top of his head. For the first time Eddie wished he hadn't worn a hat. They walked to the low cement wall that separated the apartment building from the street. Jacob Lee jumped up and sat on the wall while Eddie leaned.

Jacob Lee magically pulled a beer can out of the pocket of his cargo pants, pulled the tab, and began drinking. Eddie glanced at his watch, 11:34 a.m.

"So what about Buddy's?" Jacob said.

"You've been there on at least six different occasions when a young singer named Mari Simon was performing," Eddie said.

"Yeah," Jacob said. "And I've been there dozens of other times when other bands were playing. What about it?"

"Ms. Simon has been experiencing some problems with a stalker," Eddie said.

"Shit, you think I'm a stalker?" Jacob said. "I'm a

scout for a record label."

"You work for a record label?" Eddie said.

"Yeah," Jacob said. "Nations Roots Records in Nashville."

"That explains the wardrobe," Eddie said.

"Sure, I gotta blend in with the kids," Jacob said. "I've always had a baby face."

Eddie stifled a laugh.

"So do you know Mari Simon personally?" Eddie said.

"I've never talked to her," Jacob said. "The president of the label has been handling her. I'm just supposed to go to some shows, see the reactions, get a feel for how popular this chick can get."

"Right, well, this 'chick' seems to be very popular with at least one individual who's been sending her disturbing letters," Eddie said.

"That's great," Jacob said. "That can really help her."

"Excuse me?"

"Look at some of the stars who've had stalkers. It only helps their popularity," Jacob said. "Musicians, athletes, actors. They love having stalkers."

"I'm sure John Lennon loved having Mark David Chapman around," Eddie said.

"Sure, sometimes it ends bad," Jacob said. "But look

how famous Lennon still is."

"I'm sure it was his stalker that made him famous," Eddie said. "So have you noticed anyone at Mari Simon's shows that seemed suspicious?"

"Not that I can think of. I stick to myself, make notes, watch the crowd's reactions," Jacob said.

"You see the same people there more than once, someone who might be alone?" Eddie said.

"Yeah," Jacob said. "You."

CHAPTER 18

A ran Driscoll had killed his first man before he
turned eighteen. In the year that followed he
stopped counting. When he showed up in Belfast he was
a 16 year old kid with a blanket and a kitchen knife who
wanted to fight. The IRA didn't turn anyone away so he
became a soldier for the cause. It took him only a day
when he arrived to learn about his father and another
week to find the courage to go talk to him.

"What the hell are you doin' here, son?"
"I came to fight with you," Aran said.
"I moved you away from here so you wouldn't have to

fight," Declan said.

"Then why did you come back?" Aran said.

Declan Driscoll looked his son in the eyes.

"I lost all my friends in this fight before you were even born," Declan said. "This has been my fight since it began. It's not yours. Go home, Aran. Go home and take care of your Ma."

"No," Aran said. "I'm staying, if not with you then I'll find others who will take me in, who will train me."

First came the guns. He learned how to carry them, how to take them apart and put them back together, to clean them, and most importantly, how to shoot them. He took to the guns so fast they began to teach him about explosives and how to wire a bomb to a car in the dead of night without making a sound. Then he learned how to kill with only his hands.

Never once did he cower away from it or have a second thought. Then he stood in front of his brigade leader to learn his orders for that night.

"You're goin' in alone," his commander said. "We can't afford to lose any more men."

Aran nodded at the man and listened to the details of his mission.

Twelve miles southwest of Belfast sat Royal Air Force

base Long Kesh. Built in the Second World War to launch planes into Germany, the base was now an internment camp for captured members of the IRA under Britain's Operation Demetrius. The buildings had all been turned into makeshift cells.

With a backpack and a single loaded pistol with no extra bullets, Aran headed out after sundown. A new helipad had just been built to accommodate the large Chinook choppers that transported British troops as well as the faster Puma helicopters that their special forces utilized for attack missions. Twin fuel tanks sat a few dozen feet from the landing pad, which fed the flying beasts. Not far from the helipad stood the buildings housing 343 detained IRA fighters.

Travelling alone raised less suspicion, but Aran kept to the side roads and out of any areas where people might be out that he could. The car he drove belonged to a doctor that was friendly to their cause but would claim it stolen if it was found being used. He drove for more than an hour, circling around through neighborhoods and watched for lights behind him, then parked the car on a side road as close to the base as he safely could and set out on foot.

It took another ten minutes of walking until he reached the tall wire fence that surrounded the British base and he moved around its perimeter until he found an area of weakness where he could easily cut through the fence with the small pair of wire cutters he'd carried with him.

The helipad sat away from the buildings and lit up only when a helicopter was taking off or landing. Aran found it and stayed concealed behind a military truck while he watched for guards. In the distance he could see the dark outlines of the buildings where the men and women were being held. He'd pushed his leaders to bring more soldiers with him, to try to free them, but his mission for tonight was only to destroy the helipad.

After ten minutes he had seen no movement and decided it was clear. He set his backpack down and pulled the bombs out and placed them on the ground. He looked out at his path to the fuel tanks and the helipad, plotting his steps and calculated how long it would take him to put the explosives in place then retreat back through the camp, to the hole he'd made in the fence, then out of the reach of the searchlights. He set the timer on the bomb for ten minutes.

He patted the pistol on his side, looked up over the hood of the truck, and then walked out into the open with the bombs in his hands. Running would attract the attention of anyone that might see him much faster than a casual pace. He struggled with himself to not set off in a run, to finish the job and get out.

The lack of lights amazed him as he approached the fuel tanks and set the first bomb in the shadows at the base of the ten-foot high container. Then he turned to the helipad. The Chinook transport helicopter stood in front of him, larger than Aran had even thought they were. He stepped onto the helipad and placed his right hand on the cold metal exterior of the machine. The surface was rough, the green paint tactile beneath his fingers.

He knelt down and positioned the bomb behind the back left wheel of the helicopter then pressed the button that would start the timer.

Aran was away from the helipad and moved behind the trucks and boxes to work his way back to the hole in the fence when the cigarette smoke hit his nose. He put his hand up to cover his nostrils to keep from sneezing. Even living in close quarters for years with so many chain smokers, he had never taken to the habit, which only made him more sensitive to the smell. He stopped and knelt behind the closest object, a metal barrel. The sound came next, a man's low voice then the higher tones of a woman. He thought about going back to find better cover or an alternate route but knew it was safer to follow his same path back to the fence.

He heard the voices again then into the small clearing ahead of him came the man and woman. It was a British soldier, a cigarette hanging out of his mouth. The woman carried a bottle of whiskey and hung all over the man. She turned towards the soldier, took the cigarette out of his mouth and reached her face up towards his as he grabbed her hair roughly and kissed her, his other hand grabbed at her ass so hard it lifted her off of the ground.

"Here?" the woman said.

The soldier took a pull from the bottle.

Aran glanced at his watch, growing impatient, then looked back at the people in his way. The woman pushed away from the large soldier, placed the cigarette back in his mouth then made him lay down on the ground.

He watched from behind the barrel as she opened the soldier's pants then pulled up her short skirt and sat down on top of him, his cigarette still glowing between his lips. She moved her hips forward and backwards, slowly at first then built up speed. His hands went to her hips and began to move her faster, slamming her body into his. The woman leaned forward, grasping handfuls of the soldier's uniform on his chest in her hands, struggling to stay on top of the man as he became more and more violent with her. After a few minutes and a stifled moan, the man was finished. He pushed the woman off of him then stood and fastened his pants, leaving her lying in the dirt.

"Now get the fuck outta here," the soldier said. "Before anyone else sees you."

"What about my sister?" she climbed to her feet, pulling her skirt back down, trying to straighten it while beginning to cry. "You told me I could see my sister."

"I don't help Irish whores," the soldier said.

The woman reached back and slapped the man on the face. He turned with the slap then swung back at her with his fist and landed it on her cheek with his full weight behind it. She fell backwards to the ground.

Time was running out for Aran and he moved. He left his hiding spot behind the barrel and ran towards the soldier, keeping his steps as light as he could. He was within a few feet before the man heard him coming and turned and began to speak.

Aran never stopped running. His right arm extended and swung out.

"Who the fuck are—"

The eight-inch blade of his hunting knife came from behind his forearm as he ran and sliced through the front of the British soldier's throat. Aran was another ten feet past him before the man began to fall. He barely heard the thud of the large man as he collapsed, his hands clasped on his throat, blood spilling out onto the dark ground. The woman began to scream.

He reached the hole in the fence and paused, wondering what would happen to the girl and if he should have brought her with him. She was Irish and if found inside the fences would be thrown in with the rest of the detainees, if she wasn't shot on sight. It had been barely a minute since he killed the British soldier and the sirens began to sound and the camp lit up. He went through the fence and ran towards the darkness outside the reach of the searchlights. The girl could be a blessing or a curse. Her presence might delay their hunt for the bomber, or she might give him up quickly, pointing which way he had headed. He heard the whine of the helicopter's twin motors as the huge blades began to spin. They were going airborne to look for whoever killed their soldier. His brain began to run through how long he'd been delayed.

The bombs exploded just before the pilot lifted the aircraft off of the helipad. The left side of the helicopter disintegrated as shrapnel was thrown hundreds of feet and traveled through the bodies of a dozen more soldiers that were running towards the helipad as the alarm continued to sound. The huge machine rolled to its side and the blades dug into the dirt, the engines getting louder as the dead pilot fell forward onto the controls. The landing pad was destroyed and covered in thousands of pounds of twisted steel. The twin fuel tanks were leveled to the ground and flames lit the night sky up from the burning gas.

Aran heard movement behind him and paused.

"Please help me," she said. "They'll lock me up if they catch me, or worse."

Aran looked at her then to the direction of his car. He didn't have much time to get to it and make a safe escape.

"Just keep up with me, I'm not stopping for ya'," he said.

It took another 15 minutes to get to the car, regularly pausing to listen for sounds behind him. He got onto the main roads and headed back to Belfast. The army trucks were not far behind but their air support had been destroyed.

The girl sat beside him staring out the window, arms clutched tightly to her chest.

CHAPTER 19

Eva and Eddie cooked dinner together in her kitchen and were into their second bottle of a Pinot Noir from California. They made opportunities to bump into each other in the small galley kitchen and linger a moment, perhaps kiss, and then continue preparing their meal. Charlie Sexton Sextet's album "Under the Wishing Tree" played on the stereo in the next room.

"Before you, my homemade meals were done in two minutes with a loud beep at the end," Eddie said.

"What a shame," Eva said. "You're so good at it."

"You think so?" Eddie said.

"No," Eva said.

Eddie bumped into her again. His hands were covered with chicken and he threatened to wipe them on her blouse.

"Don't even think about it," Eva said. "Or else."

"Or else what?" Eddie said.

"Or else I'll have to take this blouse off," she said.

"You do not make a good argument," he said.

Eva leaned in and kissed Eddie on the mouth.

"How long does the chicken need in the oven?" Eva said.

"About 45 minutes," Eddie said. "Longer if you like it dried out."

"Wash your paws and meet me upstairs," Eva left the kitchen. Her blouse was off as she reached the bottom of the stairs.

Eddie watched after her until she disappeared then saw her jeans fall from the landing above. He quickly washed his hands, checked the chicken in the oven, and then ran up the stairs to find her in bed, waiting for him.

"You know, I'm kinda tired," Eddie said. "So can we just cuddle?"

"No."

Eddie grinned and went to her.

An hour later they were back in the kitchen. Eva did what she could to save the chicken as Eddie refilled their wine glasses. They sat on the floor in the living room to eat and their bodies never lost contact with each other, and they made the best of the overcooked meal.

"Any progress finding the stalker?" she said.

The discussion with Mari Simon and her French lilac scent passed through his mind. He chewed an especially tough piece of chicken and chased it with wine.

"Not too much," Eddie said. "I have the notes he's sent her and I'm going through those for any clues."

Eva giggled.

"What?" Eddie said.

"You said clues," she said. "It just sounded funny."

"Thanks," Eddie said.

"Since you need a new car maybe you could get a van like the Mystery Machine from Scooby-Doo," she said.

"Keep it up," Eddie said. "Or I'll have to not wipe chicken all over you again."

"Okay, I'm sorry," she said. "Continue telling me about your sleuthing for clues. Did you check out the owner of the abandoned amusement park?"

He looked at her out of the corner of his eye like he was irritated with her. She leaned over and kissed his cheek.

"Whoever this is that's following her," Eddie said. "He definitely has a problem. He thinks they actually know each other, that they've dated or are a couple."

"Maybe they have," Eva said.

"I think she would have told me if she was dating someone recently that might be doing this," Eddie said.

"No, the other part. Maybe they do know each other, or at least have some kind of minimal contact on occasion," Eva said. "He could be misinterpreting her friendliness as something else."

Eddie thought about Mari Simon's flirtation and the way she could look at you and make you feel like the center of a beautiful world.

"That's not bad," Eddie said. "If this whole doctoring thing doesn't work out, maybe you could be Daphne to my Fred."

"Uhh, I'd rather be Velma and you're Shaggy, at best," Eva said.

"Harsh," Eddie said.

"Do you think the bomb in your car is connected to the stalker?" Eva said.

"No, I don't," Eddie said.

"Do you know who put the bomb there?" Eva said.

"No, I don't," Eddie said. "Well, sort of."

"What do you mean?" Eva said.

Eddie had avoided telling her about the incident at the diner but knew he was going to have to eventually.

"Gus and I were shot at a couple days ago," Eddie said. "Pretty sure it was the same guy."

"You were shot at. A couple days ago. And I'm just hearing about it?" Eva said.

"You've been working for two days straight," Eddie said. "And I didn't want to worry you. We thought it was random, or were hoping it was random. Until the car thing."

"But you're going to find out who it is and make them pay," Eva said.

"Yes, I am," Eddie said.

"Good," Eva said. "I liked that car."

"Me too," Eddie said.

With dinner done and the second bottle of wine empty, they worked their way back upstairs and into her bed and made love for the second time that evening.

When they were finished they lay facing each other. The only light in the room came from the streetlights outside, filtered by the thin white curtains. Eva ran her hand down the side of Eddie's face, casting him into shadow. She felt the rough stubble on his cheeks and chin that only a few minutes earlier she had felt on her shoulder, breasts and stomach.

"I think I love you, Eddie Holland," Eva said.

The room was silent as he looked at her. He could tell

by the look in her eyes that she hadn't planned to say it. He reached his hand around her naked body under the loose sheet. The small of her back had a hint of sweat from their lovemaking.

"I know I love you, Eva Taylor," Eddie said.

CHAPTER 20

The explosion killed two people as shrapnel ripped through wood, metal and human flesh. The blast was felt more than ten miles away and the shock wave woke Eddie in Eva's bed in her neighborhood on the east side of Austin. Eddie sat up, having slept late on a Sunday morning.

"What's up?" Eva said. She rolled over and ran her hand across his chest.

"Did you feel that," Eddie said. "That rumble?"

"Quit your bragging," Eva said. "It wasn't that great."

"You didn't just feel the house shake?" Eddie said. "And really?"

"No," Eva said.

Eddie took the remote control off of the nightstand and clicked to turn on the television that was mounted on the wall across the room. He changed from station to station watching for local news but only religious programs, children's shows and channels trying to sell him unnecessary household items appeared. After ten minutes he turned the TV off.

He got out of bed and grabbed his phone and headed for the window that faced the city on the back of Eva's two-story modern styled home. Before he could dial Gus's number the phone rang in his hand. It was Gus.

"Was that what I think it was?" Eddie said.

"Sure was," Gus said. "Just off the phone with PD. It was my building."

"What?" Eddie said.

"I'm headed to the car now," Gus said.

"I'm on my way," Eddie said.

Eddie was back in the bedroom and pulled on his jeans, tee shirt with "Austin City Limits" printed on it and his running shoes. He kissed Eva and ran down the stairs. He grabbed his brown felt porkpie hat from the dining room table and was out the door within three minutes of hanging up with Gus.

Eddie sped down Martin Luther King Jr. Boulevard

then north on the highway then exited west to get to the FBI satellite field office on Research Boulevard. It had been 22 minutes since the explosion.

More than a dozen police cars blocked the ends of the road. Eddie parked the Impala and walked around the emergency vehicles and fire trucks to get to the barricades closest to the building.

"Holy shit," Eddie found Gus. "What the hell did this?"

"Too early to say for sure," Gus said. "But looks like a moving truck pulled up to the building then blew up. I heard one of the bomb techs say he thought it was C4, perhaps with a fertilizer component."

"Not an exotic explosive ordnance," Eddie said. "You can practically pick it up at the hardware store. But seing it twice in a week is strange."

"With the amount of damage here, I think it was more than a little bit of C4," Gus said. "I'm going to get some guys to start pulling traffic camera footage instead of waiting on PD. They have their hands full."

"We know of any casualties yet?" Eddie said.

"Two possibles, but we won't know until they go through the whole building," Gus said. "I had one agent who was supposed to be in the office doing some research for a trial and the IRS office downstairs is reporting one employee that was in the building also."

Gus pulled his phone out, dialed and held it to his ear. Eddie's phone rang and he stepped away from Gus and answered.

"Do ya like my little show?" the voice sang in Eddie's ear.

"Not really. I find it a bit sloppy," Eddie said. He stepped back to Gus and tapped his shoulder then pointed at the phone then at Gus's phone. Gus turned away and changed the directions to his staff to get a trace on Eddie's cellphone.

"It was," the man said. "But I wanted you to see what I can do."

"You said you were going to kill me," Eddie said. "Not innocent strangers."

"Ah, but they are your people, aren't they?" the man said. "FBI, residents of your beloved city."

"If you want to hurt me," Eddie said. "Then hurt me, not anyone else. Name the place, I'll be there."

"This is merely the prologue, Mr. Holland," the man said. "There's plenty of time before the climax of this story."

"What did I do to you?" Eddie said.

"You took from me as I'm takin' from you," the man said.

The line went dead.

Eddie turned to Gus, his ear to his phone listening as someone on the other end was tracing Eddie's phone call.

"Anything?"

"Definitely a cell, likely another burner," Gus said.

"Where?" Eddie said.

Gus listened silently, his index finger held up to tell Eddie to wait.

"Are you sure?" Gus said. "Try to continue pinging the phone to track it."

Gus hung up and casually looked around then at Eddie.

"Stay calm," Gus said.

"What?" Eddie said.

"The call went through the same tower as your phone," Gus said.

Eddie stared at Gus, trying to keep from running over to the small crowd that had gathered.

"He's here?" Eddie said.

"Looks like it," Gus said. "How do you want to play this?"

"We don't have long, he won't stand around and wait for us," Eddie said. "I'll swing around the left and grab any officers and agents I can. You go the other way to approach the crowd from both sides."

"Here, take this," Gus said. He stepped close to Eddie to block the view and pulled his Sig from its holster and handed it to him.

"I've got a backup on my ankle," Gus said.

The men walked away from each other trying their best to act casual. Eddie saw a uniformed cop he knew by name and began to lead him while giving him the short version of what they were doing. Gus had two agents by his side within a few steps of leaving Eddie.

As the two groups moved closer to the onlookers, Eddie took out his cellphone and pulled up his call history. With his finger on the send button he looked up to the crowd and pressed to dial the last number that had called him.

He looked at Gus, thirty feet away, who was acting as if he were chatting with his agents as he watched Eddie. The muffled beeping of a cellphone ringer sounded near the back of the group and everyone moved as Eddie and Gus ran towards the sound. Guns out, the officers and agents pushed the civilians out of the group, some to the ground, as they cleared the way to find the sound before it stopped.

Gus stopped and turned to see Eddie with his pistol raised and aimed at the face of a tall, lean man. Gus raised his weapon and moved around behind the man and motioned for the officers and agents to take up a perimeter.

The man stared at Eddie and his hands came up from his sides until they were in the air over his head.

"Hands on the back of your head and down to your knees," Gus said.

The man looked at Gus then to his left and right and back at Eddie.

"What the hell is happening?" the man said.

In a smooth movement Gus had his gun holstered as he stepped forward and had his handcuffs on the man's wrists then doubled him over and put him face down on the ground.

"What are you doing?" the man yelled. "I didn't do anything!"

Eddie moved his hand under the man's shoulders then to his sides, hips and then to his back jeans pockets. His hands stopped as he was patting then reached into the right rear pocket and pulled out a cheap flip phone.

He rolled the man over and shoved the phone in his face.

"Is this yours?" Eddie said.

"What? No," the man said. "My phone's in my front pocket. Who the hell carries a flip phone anymore?"

Eddie patted the man's front pockets and found a thin smart phone.

"Let him go," Eddie stood and walked away, the phone in his hands, and Gus joined him as his agents helped the man up.

"He must have slipped it into the guy's pocket," Eddie said. "He was right here, dammit."

Gus held out a plastic bag and Eddie dropped the phone in.

"I'm sure he wore gloves or wiped it down, but we'll check it out," Gus said.

CHAPTER 21

E ddie was up early the next morning and running in the crisp air. He processed the day before in his mind. He'd worked anti-terrorism for more than a decade and had seen more than his share of destruction, but never in his hometown. At first his enemies had always been faces of men pinned to the wall, living in remote villages and caves on the other side of the world. Then he was recruited for a new team within the task force and began going on clandestine ground operations on foreign soil, seeing his enemies face to face. Even through those missions he'd never lost a team member. Agents die in the line of duty, but none had died in any case related to him.

He was into his tenth mile before he let his thoughts move over to Mari Simon. He'd gone through the box of notes from the stalker and was becoming more concerned for her safety.

Showered and dressed he drove across town and found Mari in her usual spot on the sofa at the coffee shop.

"Any more notes?" Eddie said.

"No, it's been quiet," Mari said. "But I also haven't had a gig in a few days. Don't know if that's related."

"You know someone named Jacob Lee?" Eddie said.

"No, should I?" Mari said.

"He works for Nations Roots Records," Eddie said.

"I've talked with another guy there," Mari said. "Malcolm Evers. He came out from Nashville once to see a show then took me to dinner after to talk about a record deal."

"Anything come from it?" Eddie said.

"It looked promising. I really thought I was going to get a contract," Mari said. "But after I shut him down that night, nothing ever came from it."

"Shut him down?" Eddie said. "He made a pass?"

"If you can call it that," she said. "He clumsily tried to kiss me in the back of a cab. Sad thing is I think he thought he was being smooth."

"Ahh, romance," Eddie said. "So you think you didn't get a deal because of that? He seem like the kind of guy to hold a grudge?"

"If you're wondering if he could be the stalker, I really don't think so," she said. "I thought about him early on, but he runs the record label and rumor has it only leaves Nashville for new acts if they are young and female."

"What a gentleman," Eddie said.

"Not everyone can be as valiant as you," Mari said.

"I had a thought," Eddie said. "From the last note where he mentioned smelling you. There's a chance it's someone you may know, not closely, but that you are perhaps in contact with at times. Someone who gets close enough to, well, smell you."

"Wow, that makes this even creepier," Mari said.

"I agree, and potentially more dangerous," Eddie said. "This could be someone who could get very close to you without you feeling threatened."

"You really know how to make a girl feel good," Mari said.

"I'm just trying to prepare you," Eddie said. "You have to be aware of everything around you, everyone around you."

"So am I supposed to take notes on everyone I come

in contact with?" Mari said.

"If it helps. It wouldn't seem out of character since you're always writing in your notebook," Eddie said. "Just think of it as research for a song. Notice the people around you, how they act and treat you."

"Okay," Mari said. "Can I call you?"

"What?" Eddie said.

"If anything comes up, if I'm feeling uncomfortable about someone," Mari said. "Or if I just wanna talk?"

Eddie took a moment. "If you're feeling uncomfortable about someone, yes. If you are feeling threatened dial 911."

"I have a gig at Buddy's tonight, if you want to come," Mari said.

"I think that can work," Eddie said. "But don't put me on the list. I want to hang back and watch the crowd."

"Oh, what happened to your cute old car?" Mari said. "I saw you pull up in an unmarked police car. I really wanted to go for a ride in your convertible."

Eddie looked out the window and shook his head.

"It's just a rental," he said. "My Karmann Ghia stopped running."

EDDIE SAT AT a table in the window of the cafe across the street from his sister's office building in downtown

Austin. He was half an hour early on purpose, to sit and think without distraction. He finished a club sandwich and fries. After a swig of water he glanced at his watch and motioned to the waitress.

"Shiner, please," he said.

"Sure thing," the waitress said.

The beer arrived and he savored the first sip like it was a fine wine. His stress levels were currently close to some of his most hectic days in Washington D.C. and were the reason he left the bureau to return home to Texas.

"Where are you?" Shelley said.

Eddie looked up and his sister was seated across from him, her hands waving at him.

"What?" Eddie said.

"I come in, pull out my chair and sit at the table without you even noticing," Shelley said. "Some supercop you are."

Eddie didn't know where to begin.

"The FBI building blew up yesterday morning."

"I heard something about it on the news," Shelley said. "Gus is okay isn't he? They weren't giving much in the way of details. Was it a gas leak?"

"No," Eddie said. "It's someone trying to get to me. A few days ago my car was wired with explosives. Before that he took a shot at Gus and me at the diner from eight blocks away. He's playing with me, doesn't want me dead yet."

Shelley leaned back in her seat and looked out the window. A garbage truck stopped in front of the café blocking any view.

"Do I need to be worried about my kids again?" Shelley said.

Eddie drank from the beer bottle.

"I can't put you in protection," he said. "I wouldn't, not with things as tense as they already are with me and Samuel."

"I feel a 'but' coming on," Shelley said.

"But…" Eddie said. "If you have any vacation time, heading to Disneyworld wouldn't be a bad idea."

"Shit," Shelley said.

Shelley motioned to the waitress and pointed at Eddie's bottle.

"Don't you have to go back to work?" Eddie said.

"My boss is out plus nobody cares," she said. "The partners come back from lunch reeking of bourbon and cigar smoke."

Her beer came and she pulled down a third of the bottle.

"Sis still has it after all these years," Eddie said.

"That's about all I got from my sorority days," she said. "I think I can get Samuel to go for a trip. It's short notice, but I'll tell him I got a really good deal. He likes deals."

"Thanks," Eddie said. "I'll feel a lot better with you safely out of town."

"I can only go for a week at most," Shelley said.

"I have to take this guy down faster than that so he doesn't rack up a bigger body count," Eddie said. "Fly as soon as you can."

"What about Eva?" Shelley said.

"She has several shifts in a row the next few days so she'll be at the hospital most of the time. I'll put in a call and get some extra security around the building and inside," Eddie said.

They finished their beers.

"You're lucky," Eddie said. "You have the kids. And Samuel, I guess."

"You have Eva," Shelley said.

"It's not the same," Eddie said. "Most of our lives it was just you, me and dad. You were a little older when mom died, but I have trouble remembering much about her."

"I didn't think it bothered you," Shelley said. "Having a small family."

"Dad was barely there for us. I see him in my mirror more everyday and wonder if I'd be like him," he said.

"What, with kids?" Shelley said. "Baby brother, you don't know how good it feels to hear you even think about children."

"Don't get ahead of yourself," Eddie said.

"The way you are with your niece and nephew, I think you'd be great," Shelley said.

"Anything like that is a long way off, if at all," Eddie said. "And... change of topic, please."

The two drank from their beer bottles.

"So what about your job for Father Dom?" Shelley said.

"I'm hot on the trail of Mari's stalker," Eddie said.

"So you're close to catching him," she said.

"God no. I have no clue who it is," he said. "I'm hoping maybe it's the bomber so I can solve two cases at once."

"Not funny," she said.

"I know."

"I'm glad we finally got to meet Eva," Shelley said. "I didn't scare her off too bad, did I?"

"She doesn't scare easy," he said. "Which is obvious since she's hung around me for a year."

"I figured that. I like her," she said. "So..."

"So… no pressure please," he said. "I have enough going on right now."

Shelley smiled at her baby brother.

"I'm just happy to see you happy," she said. "As far as I know this is your longest relationship since high school. Other than Gus, of course."

"What Gus and I have is special."

"Nice," she said. "So after we come back from hiding out in Florida we'll have you two over for dinner, let her meet the kids."

"What did I say about no pressure?" he said.

CHAPTER 22

Eddie was standing in line to get coffee when his phone beeped. He glanced at it and read the text message: "Get to Research Blvd when you can."

He texted back: "Be there in 10 min with coffee." After buying two large cups of coffee he continued on to the FBI office.

Eddie arrived at the building and found Gus working out of the mobile command center vehicle that had come up from the San Antonio field office. Gus was on the phone when Eddie stepped in through the door into the back of the van and he set one of the coffees in front of him.

"Yes, Director," Gus said. "I appreciate the call. I'll let you know if we need anything."

Gus hung up and turned to Eddie with a stunned look.

"Director?" Eddie said.

"Yes," Gus said. "I just got off the phone with the Director of the FBI. He offered anything we need to take care of business and find who did this."

"That's huge," Eddie said.

"Yes it is," Gus said. "But right now we have a video briefing from the lab at Quantico. The bomb fragments from the U-Haul and your car were flown out to them."

Another agent in the van was making the secure connections and brought up video from the lab halfway across the country. A woman in the traditional white lab coat appeared on screen with two men in the background.

"Special Agent Ramirez," she said. "I'm Dr. Rebecca Stoddard, pleasure to meet you."

"Likewise," Gus said to the screen. "Thank you for putting a rush on this for us."

"One of our own is dead," Dr. Stoddard said. "Even if I hadn't put a rush on it, there were several phone calls from DC insisting on it."

"I'm sure there were. IRS is very involved as well,"

Gus said. "This is Eddie Holland, he's consulting with us."

"Yes, we've met," Dr. Stoddard said. "Eddie, it's good to see you, especially now. I believe your background is going to be especially helpful."

"Thanks, Becca," Eddie said. "Great to see you, too."

Gus glanced at Eddie, unsurprised that he'd at some time during his tenure at the Washington Field Office had worked with Dr. Stoddard, but impressed he was close enough to the stunning woman to call her Becca.

"There are similarities between the two devices," she said. "I can say they were most definitely built by the same person. The wiring on the detonators in particular was identical."

"That at least proves the explosions were connected," Gus said. "Not that we had any doubt."

"The device on the car was basic," Dr. Stoddard said. "It had all of the components, it just wasn't connected to the starter. The bomb couldn't have gone off."

"Now you tell me," Eddie said.

"Now the device at your office," Dr. Stoddard said. "That was simple, brute force."

"How's that?" Gus said.

"The primary explosive component was C4, and a lot of it," she said. "But there was a large amount of ammonium nitrate fertilizer added to increase the yield."

"It took down half the building," Gus said. "What does that mean for us?" Gus said.

"It means it might be far harder to trace," Eddie said. "C4 is used on almost every military base and by bomb squads across the country. So it might be explosives missing from some ordnance lockup or it could have been stolen from a construction company that does demolition work."

"It's something to start with," Gus said. "Thank you."

"Anytime," Dr. Stoddard said. "And Eddie, let me know next time you're back in DC."

"Will do," Eddie said.

Gus hit the button to end the videoconference and turned to Eddie.

"Don't forget you have a girlfriend now," Gus said.

"You think she was flirting?" Eddie said. "She was talking about C4 and explosions."

"To you, that's flirting," Gus said. He turned in his chair to face Eddie. "Got something else, didn't want to bring it up on the call."

"What's up?" Eddie said.

"They were able to get a serial number off the axle of the U-Haul truck," Gus said. "Tracked it to a rental firm in Huntsville, Alabama. Was rented four days ago by an

Army Corporal from Redstone Arsenal."

"Is the soldier Irish?" Eddie said.

"Nope," Gus said. A photograph of Hector Castellano appeared on the screen.

"What's the connection then?" Eddie said.

"When we began running the Corporal's name, we got a hit in Texas," Gus said. "His body has just been identified in a rental car explosion in Hillsboro, just south of Dallas."

"C4?" Eddie said.

"Prelim says the gas tank was ignited by a line from the spark plug," Gus said.

"A U-Haul leaves Alabama and drives to Texas, then the driver ends up dead in a rental car," Eddie said. "You have an ID on who rented the car?"

"Sure do," Gus said. "Jason Sutherland. Lives in Portland, Oregon. At the time the car blew up, he was on an airplane headed from Dallas back to Portland."

"The corporal was driving from Redstone to Texas," Eddie said. "Our C4 had to come from Redstone."

"That's exactly what I'm thinking," Gus said.

"I'm going to go see Clem," Eddie said. "See if he can be any help."

"I'll drive," Gus said.

"I was hoping you'd say that," Eddie said.

CHAPTER 23

The drive to Fort Hood was quiet in Gus's SUV. Eddie slept, his head rested on the side window. He woke just as they slowed to enter the Army post.

"Thanks for keeping me company," Gus said.

"Figured you could use some quiet time," Eddie said.

"You snore," Gus said.

Gus pulled up to the guard station at Fort Hood. The two men cleared their credentials through the solider on duty and they drove onto the post and wound around to the building that housed the training faciliity run by Clem Akins. They parked next to a restored Korean War era army Jeep with the canvas top up and headed inside.

"Eddie Holland," the voice boomed from the building.

Eddie and Gus walked into the building as Clem Akins came out of his office. Eddie and Clem wrapped their arms around each other in a firm grip and held it several moments.

"I can leave if you two want to be alone," Gus said.

The two men separated and the tall black army Major turned to Gus.

"So you must be Gus Ramirez," Clem said.

Clem and Gus shook hands.

"I feel I know you. I can't believe it took Eddie this long to bring you up to my playground," Clem said.

"Unfortunately we're not here to play today," Eddie said.

Clem ran a training facility for the soldiers that came through Fort Hood that was unique from any other post. Having been an Army Ranger before losing a leg in Afghanistan he liked to train all of the men and women as if they were part of the elite squad. The building housed everything from a wrestling mat, obstacle course and a live fire gun range.

"That's too bad," Clem said. "I had some new tricks ready for you."

"Tempting, but we really don't have the time," Eddie said.

"Your loss," Clem said. "So what can I do for the FBI today?"

The men went into Clem's office and poured coffee for themselves. They sat on the old leather sofa and the recliner that Clem had claimed when the post had updated its enlisted men's recreation center.

"We're looking for C4," Gus said.

"Okay," Clem said. "I have about twenty pounds in storage downstairs."

"Well, we're actually looking for missing C4," Eddie said.

"Is this about the explosion in Austin?" Clem said.

"Sure is. And my car was wired with a few pounds of it," Eddie said.

"About time you got a real car anyway," Clem said. "So you're trying to track the explosives?"

"Indeed," Gus said. "It was C4 at both, though wrapped in fertilizer at the FBI office. We're hoping to see if any has gone missing from military facilities."

"Most of the units will use C4 and keep some on hand," Clem said.

"Is it hard to acquire?" Gus said.

"Sadly, not at all," Clem said. "Especially at larger facilities. We keep just enough for small training procedures, but larger posts will have a lot of it. And a missing pound or two is hardly noticeable."

"What about larger amounts?" Eddie said. "We can't assume this guy only had enough for two jobs."

"You think it came from the army?" Clem said.

"No, it could just as easily have come from a police or FBI bomb squad, or even a demolition company," Eddie said. "But we have some information that may tie this to Alabama."

Clem leaned back and looked out the window.

"Off the record, boys," Clem said. "But unofficially there has been rumor of some materials going missing from Redstone."

Gus and Eddie looked at each other then back at Clem. Redstone Arsenal is an army post with more than thirty thousand staff from military, FBI, DEA and other government agencies, and it's where Hector Castellano had been posted.

"If you're military and into explosive ordnance, you end up at Redstone at some point in your career," Clem said. "I spent six months there before Afghanistan. It's the largest supply of the stuff you can find in one place."

"How much is rumored to be missing," Gus said.

"Again, only rumors, but a lot," Clem said. "Hundreds of pounds, if not more, as well as blasting caps, automatic weapons, sniper rifles and anything else you might need to wage a small war."

"Or a big one," Eddie said.

"I can make some calls, if you like," Clem said. "See if I can find out any more."

"No, don't need you raising any red flags," Gus said. "Last thing we need is the Army coming to Austin to hunt for their missing ordnance."

CHAPTER 24

The house was full at Buddy's for Mari Simon's show. She came on after a forty-five minute opening set by a band of three guys from Dallas. The crowd was friendly to the opening act but when Mari stepped on stage they became focused, almost reverent to her.

She played for an hour then said she was taking a short break and would be back. Her band members went backstage to relax in the dressing room, have a few drinks and a smoke. Mari stepped down to the front of the stage where a waitress handed her a warm water with lemon and she talked to anyone who came up to her.

Aran Driscoll watched as she sipped her water and listened to a freshman from the university talk about being a business major and wishing she could do what Mari does instead. After the girl hugged her and stepped away, Aran walked up to her.

"Ms. Simon," he said. "I've never heard ya' before tonight but I must say I love what I hear."

Mari smiled and brushed her hair out of her face with her hand.

"Thank you so much," she said. "And I love your accent. Irish?"

"Indeed," he said. "You've got a good ear."

"I've always wanted to visit Ireland," Mari said.

"And you should. It's a glorious place with the friendliest people on earth," he reached his hand out. "Sean. Sean O'Doole."

"You even have an O," she said.

She took his hand and he placed his other hand on top of hers.

"All the best Irish do," he said.

"I'm Mari, but I guess you probably already knew that," she said.

"Would you do me the pleasure of going for a cup of tea sometime?" Aran said.

CHAPTER 25

E ddie stared at a photograph of Aran Driscoll on a large screen in the FBI command center van.

"There's not too many Irish mercenaries," Gus said.

"So you think this is him?" Eddie said.

"Quantico says it is," Gus said. "The voice on your phone was almost a perfect match, but the last recording of him was 15 years ago and analog from a payphone in Stockholm."

They looked at the picture then Gus switched to a screen that told Aran Driscoll's story, as much as it was known.

"Mercenary, eh?" Eddie said.

"There's more than two dozen kills attributed to him since 2001, and that's just what they've pinned on him."

"What about before 2001? Where was he?" Eddie said.

"Irish record keeping in the 80s and 90s was rare and a lot still hasn't been computerized from the small towns," Gus said. "But the general thought is that he was with the IRA."

"So we have a name and a face," Eddie said. "And he appears to be a truly bad guy. But why me?"

"I can't answer that one for you," Gus said. "But there's more."

Gus tapped a key and a new photo came up of a man twenty years older than Aran.

"Declan Driscoll," Gus said.

"Aran's father?" Eddie said.

"Yup. And even less information is available on him than his son, except that he was a known IRA officer for nearly 15 years."

"So it ran in the family," Eddie said. "Anything on where he is now?"

"Nothing," Gus said. "He went off the grid around 2001 and is presumed dead."

"That's not too surprising. Let me know if you get anything else. I'm going to follow up with my old boss."

Eddie left the van and drove down through Austin in his rented Impala. He picked up lunch from a food truck on South Congress then parked and walked to his favorite bench overlooking Town Lake. After eating, he wiped his hands with the napkins and stuffed all the trash into the brown paper bag his food had come in and set it beside him.

He pulled out his phone and dialed.

"Olson," the voice on the other end said.

"Ben, it's Eddie."

"Eddie fuckin' Holland, how the hell are you?" His former boss from the Joint Terrorism Task Force in DC leaned back in his desk chair.

"Livin' the dream," Eddie said. "How's the Hoover building treating you?"

"Sucks as always," Ben said. "This building could drain the life out of anyone."

"Glad to hear you're happy then," Eddie said.

"Wouldn't have it any other way," Ben said. "I'm not out there getting shot at anymore. But I'm betting you aren't calling to shoot the shit."

"I wish I were," Eddie said. "I need access to JTTF files from my days there."

"I'm not with the Joint Terrorism Task Force anymore," Ben said. "And you haven't been active for almost two years."

"No, but it's important," Eddie said. "Got someone from my past trying to make me dead."

"That's pretty important unless you don't mind being dead," Ben said.

"I mind very much," Eddie said.

"Still, pretty hard to release classified docs to a civilian," Ben said.

Eddie lowered the phone to his lap for a moment as he stared up at the clouds, contemplating whether to push his luck.

"We have full support of the Director's office, Ben," Eddie said. "I'm sure you heard about our incident down here."

"Of course. Nobody takes the death of one of our own lightly," Ben said. "Tell you what, I have a batch of new agents fresh out of Quantico assigned to me. I'm supposed to be getting them up to speed to move over to counterintelligence."

"Yeah?" Eddie said. He hoped he knew where Ben was headed.

"Why don't I set this up as a test research project? Six eager to impress rookies will be able to go through far more data than a couple of you down there."

"That would be great," Eddie said. The men talked

more about what Eddie was looking for and he shared what few details he had on Aran Driscoll.

"I'll keep you in the loop and let you know anything we find that might help," Ben said.

CHAPTER 26

E ddie parked his rental car in the hospital parking lot and entered through the emergency room exit just past midnight. A nurse at the check-in desk saw him and pointed towards the door that led to a long hallway, and the doctor's lounge.

"There you are," he said.

"There you are, too," Eva said. "I feel like I haven't seen you in days."

Eva stood from the small table where her late night lunch was set out in several plastic containers and held Eddie to her body, arms tight around his neck.

"Any luck yet?" she said.

"Not yet, but I think we may be onto something."

"I want this over," Eva said. "I can't handle knowing some guy is out there wanting to kill you."

"Would you rather I hadn't told you?" he said.

"No. I'd want to know," Eva said. "If something happened, I'd want to know why it happened without waiting on official reports. And since I'm not family they'd never tell me anyway."

"You know Gus would tell you what you needed to know," he said.

"Gus would probably be with you," Eva said.

"True," Eddie said. "Looks like you have a gourmet meal for yourself here. If you're feeding a rabbit."

"I hate eating heavy on the late shift," Eva said. "Hard enough to stay awake without weighing myself down with food."

"I totally understand," Eddie said.

"You smell like pizza," Eva said.

"It was a light pizza," Eddie said.

"Right," Eva said.

They sat at the table while Eva picked at her salad and various other vegetables.

"How's Mari?" Eva said.

"Fine, as far as I know," Eddie said. "I followed up on one lead but don't think anything came of it."

"Don't think?" Eva said. "That doesn't sound like my little super sleuth."

"Okay. I'm pretty sure nothing came of it," Eddie said. "There was a guy at a lot of her shows, turned out to be a record label rep."

"How many shows has he been to?" Eva said.

"Six that I know of."

"Hmm," Eva said.

"Hmm, what?" Eddie said.

"Just seems odd he'd keep going back to the same performer over and over," Eva said. "It's not like we don't have a lot of music in the city."

"Can't throw a rock," Eddie said.

"Exactly," Eva said.

"Maybe I'll call the label in Nashville, check him out," Eddie said.

"You haven't yet?" Eva said.

"You want me to stay here and doctor people while you go look for a stalker?" Eddie said.

"No, I think it's a better idea if I stay here and doctor people, as you say," Eva said.

"Their loss," Eddie said.

"Doubtful," Eva said.

Eddie looked around the room at the vending machines and coffee maker then down at the floor.

"What is it?" Eva said.

"What do you mean?" Eddie said.

"You want to say something," Eva said.

"Damn, you're good. You sure you don't want to become a private detective?" Eddie said.

"So what is it," Eva said.

"I've been thinking," Eddie said. "Seems kinda silly for us to have separate places."

Eva set her fork down and picked up her napkin and dabbed the corners of her mouth then set the napkin back down and then looked up at Eddie.

"Seriously?" Eva said. "One o'clock in the morning in my hospital break room while I'm eating a salad I made eight hours ago is when you bring up moving in together?"

"Sure," Eddie said. "Seemed like the perfect time."

"You get out of here so I can finish eating and get back to work," Eva said. "Because right now I can't tell if I want to strangle you or drag you into an empty room and have my way with you."

"Do I get to choose?"

"You don't," Eva said.

CHAPTER 27

The alarm went off at eight o'clock and Eddie rolled over, turned it off, and slept for another fifteen minutes before getting up and dressed for a run. He stopped at the front door, hand on the doorknob, then went back to his bed and picked up his cellphone off of the side table and typed out a text message.

"Aran Driscoll, how about we meet up and chat about our little situation."

He reread the message three times before sending it to the last number he had for the killer. The burner phone the man had used was likely in a trashcan or at the bottom of Ladybird Lake by now, but it was all he had. He put the phone down and went out the front door and ran for ninety minutes.

The phone beeped in his pocket and Aran Driscoll pulled it out and read the message on the screen. It was the first time a target had ever identified him. He put the phone down beside him and looked out the car window.

He watched as Eddie Holland came out the front of his apartment building and began jogging down the sidewalk then crossed the street a few cars in front of him. By the end of the block Eddie had picked up speed and turned the corner out of view.

After the fighting with England ended, Aran followed his father into new work with their old skills. He had been a kid who joined a fight and ended up a man with no experience in anything but killing. In 1999 he found himself in an empty office in Munich.

The sun was low and shadows ran long through the city streets. He lay prone on the worn carpet, the barrel of his rifle extended only a few inches out a three-inch hole he'd cut in the window on the thirteenth floor. Through the scope on top of the long weapon he watched the front door of a luxury residential tower six blocks down the street.

He controlled his breathing while he waited. His watch sat propped on the window to the right of the hole so he could watch the time.

"8:30," he said. "Time for dinner."

A moment later the front door of the building opened. Two men came out, looked each direction then one motioned back to the door. A round man came out with a bodyguard on either side. Aran squeezed the trigger.

The bullet left Aran Driscoll's rifle and struck the German man in the forehead as he stepped to the sidewalk. Aran continued to watch through the scope on the high-powered weapon to see the man's guards pull their weapons and begin scanning for the shooter. He dismantled the rifle and put the parts into the tennis bag beside him, complete with racquet sticking out of the side pocket. He went down the twelve flights of stairs then walked down the street, past the site of the shooting and kept walking as the first police car came down the road with its siren blaring.

Half a day later Aran sat in a large, comfortable leather chair in an office in Geneva, Switzerland. He had a black coffee in his hand and a view of the lake through the window.

"Thank you for waiting, Mr. Driscoll," a man walked into the office from a different door than Aran had entered through. "I'm William White."

"Pleasure," Aran stood to shake the man's hand then sat back down and took note of the accent.

He watched the man take a seat behind the large wooden desk. The surface was bare except for a single piece of paper that was centered in front of him. His suit looked custom tailored and very expensive.

"You're British," Aran said.

"Will that be a problem?" Mr. White said. "I assure you I was on neither side of the conflicts that kept you busy for many years."

Aran sat quietly and stared at the man then took a sip of his coffee.

"So, Mr. Driscoll," Mr. White said. "I commend you on your work in Munich yesterday. It was very clean and very fast."

"Thank you, sir," Aran said.

"How were you able to accomplish the task so quickly?" Mr. White said. "I didn't expect you to complete your test for at least a week. Most of my contractors take at least that long to track a target's movements and build a workable scenario before finalizing the contract."

"Finalizing the contract?" Aran said. "Is that lawyer speak for killing a man?"

Mr. White put his fingertips together, elbows

suspended in the air on an imaginary surface.

"This is a job. We get hired by important and wealthy people to do messy things," Mr. White said. "Any bit of civility we can bring to the work, we do."

"Right. Well, to finalize this man's life," Aran said. "I didn't need a week to track his movements. The first day I saw him and his security I knew they wouldn't be any problem to get through."

"And why is that?" Mr. White said.

"They were contractors, they had no buy-in to the man," Aran said. "All I needed was one bullet to get past them then they're checked out. Their job was to protect. Once the man is dead, they have no job to do anymore."

"What's the difference between them and you then?" Mr. White said. "You're all contractors."

"I'm on the other end of the gun," Aran said. "My job isn't to protect. It's to kill."

Aran thought he saw surprise in the stoic man's face. Even in this world of hired killers, such bluntness was unexpected.

"Indeed," Mr. White said. "And speaking of that, I must mention that not all assignments can be accomplished with a sniper's rifle."

"I'm good at any distance," Aran said.

"I have no problem believing that," Mr. White said.

"You come very highly recommended, though I doubt your own father would say anything bad about you."

"There's days he would," Aran said.

"I am personally hesitant to bring you on. You are rough, uncivilized and a possible weak link in our cadre of professionals," Mr. White said. "But sometimes there are jobs that don't necessarily require a soft touch and a smooth tongue."

"I never claimed to be Sean Connery," Aran said. "But I can do whatever needs to be done."

The British man sat back in his chair and turned to look out the window at Lake Geneva. The surface of the water was smooth and reflected the mountains in a perfect mirror image. Aran waited and watched the man. It was five minutes before White turned back to him and spoke again.

"You will make a lot of money, very quickly," Mr. White said. "You must learn how to handle your money in a discreet manner, how to live without drawing attention to yourself, and not have any friends or relationships who might raise questions about your profession."

"I got my Da to talk to and will have money to pay for women when I want them," Aran said. "I don't need friends."

"Very well," Mr. White said. "We will set up a bank account for you in town for your operating money. You will be provided a method of contacting your handler whenever necessary. You are never to return to this office again and will likely never speak with me again."

"William White even your real name?" Aran said.

The man smiled at him.

"Some jobs will have deadlines, others may be more open ended, depending on the complexity of the target," Mr. White said. "Your handler will arrange travel and weapons as needed."

"Will I meet my handler?" Aran said.

"No," Mr. White said.

"Of course not," Aran said.

"Frequency of assignments vary, but you can generally expect no more than one per month," Mr. White said. "During the busy seasons at least."

"Busy seasons?" Aran said.

"Elections, Mr. Driscoll," he said.

Aran nodded.

"Welcome aboard, Mr. Driscoll," Mr. White said. He stood and reached his hand across the desk.

Aran stood and shook his hand then left the office and the building. An hour later he was on an airplane leaving Geneva and headed towards Dublin.

CHAPTER 28

Mari Simon stood on stage, her Martin guitar hung from her neck. Her eyes were closed as she sang into the microphone. Eddie stood in the back of the full house and found it hard to concentrate on anything but the music.

"I'm glad you talked me into this," Gus said. "I feel like I've been locked in that damn van."

"You have," Eddie said.

"Any progress finding her stalker?" Gus said.

"Other than now knowing the words to most of her songs, no," Eddie said. "But she hasn't gotten a note in a few days now."

"Maybe he gave up," Gus said.

"We're never that lucky," Eddie said.

"I'll be right back," Gus said. "My resistance is low."

Gus set his beer on the rail behind him and walked around the back of the standing crowd that circled the dozen tables in front of the stage. He pushed the heavy wooden bathroom door open with his elbow and went to the furthest wall urinal, unzipped, and stood staring at the wall where the cover of the sports section from the newspaper was tacked to a bulletin board.

Mari's voice came through the walls and Gus listened as he waited for his body to work. He didn't look over his shoulder when the door opened then closed behind him.

Gus looked down to shake off and zip. A hand grabbed the back of his head and smashed his face into the wall above the urinal. His hand instinctively reached to his right hip but his gun was locked in the glove box of his SUV outside.

As he began to turn he was shoved forward against the cold and wet porcelain urinal. His head was pulled back again by his hair, his left leg was knocked out from under him and his forehead was pounded into the drain of the urinal. The blood that ran down his face and into his eyes blurred his vision. His head rested in the cold water and his own piss. He tried to move his arms, to throw an elbow backwards but had no force behind. A knee landed a solid blow into his ribs. He collapsed onto the floor.

The man behind him knelt and pulled Gus's head off the floor.

"Tell Eddie hello for me."

Gus's head was dropped back to the floor and he heard the bathroom door open and close before he passed out.

CHAPTER 29

E va stood beside Gus's bed in the hospital and watched his vital signs on the monitor. It had been six hours since he was brought in during her shift in the emergency room and the sun was just starting to brighten the window at the end of the room.

"Anything?" Eddie came through the door.

"Not yet," Eva said. "Everything is stable but he hasn't woken up yet. But he will. He's strong."

"I know," Eddie said.

"MRI showed a concussion but no hemorrhaging in his skull," Eva said. "He's lucky."

Eddie stood on the other side of the bed and looked at

his friend's face. The blood had been cleaned up, but the bruising covered half his head and the swelling nearly closed off his left eye. Half of his scalp had been shaved to the skin to allow the doctors to sew him up. A cut ran across his forehead from the collision with the urinal.

"What happened?" Eva said.

"He went to the bathroom," Eddie said. "He was gone too long. Then I saw a couple guys from the bar running to the bathroom. I got a bad feeling and I followed them."

"Any idea who did this to him?" Eva said.

"No," Eddie said. "Unless it's the Irishman."

"Another way of hurting you?" Eva said.

"Most likely," Eddie said. "Now why don't you go get some rest? You worked all night."

"I don't want to drive home," Eva said.

"Then go to the doctors' lounge, at least get an hour or two of sleep."

She looked at Gus's broken face and lightly touched the side of his head.

Eva left the room and Eddie sat in the chair beside the bed. He checked his phone but found no messages and no missed calls. He'd already called the Special Agent in Charge out of the San Antonio field office. By now everyone knew not to contact Gus until further notice.

When there was nothing left to distract Eddie he looked at Gus's face. He glanced at the closed room door and then back to the bed and reached out and took Gus's hand.

"What the hell, Gus," he said. "Bad things aren't supposed to happen to you."

He continued to hold Gus's hand even after the waiting wore him out and he fell asleep in the chair, his head resting on the side of the bed.

Eddie and Gus met in third grade but they didn't become friends for a few more years. From then on they were inseparable. They played high school football together, went on double dates, to college, then eventually to become FBI agents at Quantico in Virginia. After their sixteen-week training they were assigned to different offices. Through their separation they talked often but saw each other in person rarely. Eddie was fast tracked into counterintelligence while Gus was assigned to organized crime in Chicago.

Eddie woke up from what felt like hours of sleep and looked at Gus, hoping to see his eyes open, but they weren't. His hand was sweaty from holding Gus's but he didn't want to let go. He glanced at his watch. It had been only forty-five minutes since Eva left to get some sleep.

"Come on, buddy," Eddie said.

The door opened behind him and he pulled his hand away.

"Keeping him warm?" Eva said.

"Saw that, huh?" Eddie said.

"Yes, and it was very sweet," Eva said. "Human contact has been shown to help people recover from traumatic injury."

"Yeah, I knew that. That's why I was holding his hand," Eddie said.

Eva smiled and hugged Eddie.

"We've known each other a long time," Eddie said.

"So do you think you can do a better job keeping him from getting the shit kicked out of him?" Eva said.

"I'll try," Eddie said.

Eddie slept beside the bed, his head on his arm as it rested on the mattress. He'd been out four hours when he felt movement beside him and looked up.

Gus's eyes were open, staring at the ceiling.

"Gus, it's Eddie," he said. "Can you hear me?"

He stood and leaned over the bed. Gus gradually brought his eyes over and met Eddie's before he spoke.

"Can you tell me about the rabbits, George?" Gus said.

"Of course I can, Lenny," Eddie said.

Gus began to laugh and Eddie saw him struggle to stop as the pain hit his head again.

"Hit this button," Eddie said. "That'll give you some good drugs."

Gus pushed the button on the remote to deliver a dose of morphine into his body.

"What the hell happened to me?" Gus said.

"I'd love to say 'you should see the other guy,'" Eddie said. "But you are the other guy. Do you know who it was?"

"Yeah," Gus said. "It was Driscoll."

"Dammit," Eddie said. "He was right there in the bar."

"He followed me into the restroom," Gus said. "I never had a chance."

"You'll get your chance," Eddie said.

CHAPTER 30

E ddie Holland sat on his bench overlooking Town Lake and dialed the number he'd found online and waited as it rang.

"Nations Roots Records," a woman's voice answered.

"Malcolm Evers, please," Eddie said.

"I'm sorry, Mr. Evers doesn't take calls or meetings without an appointment," she said. "May I take a message?"

"Please tell Mr. Evers that Special Agent Eddie Holland with the Federal Bureau of Investigation would like to speak with him immediately," Eddie gave the woman his phone number and hung the phone up without saying anything else.

He looked out over the skyline of Austin and enjoyed the warmth from the sun that fought through the cool breeze coming off of the water. His phone rang.

"Eddie Holland," he answered.

"Agent Holland, this is Malcolm Evers. How can I help you?"

"Thank you for getting back to me so quickly," Eddie said. "I'm in Austin, Texas and am looking into a case involving Mari Simon. Are you familiar with her?"

The phone was silent for a moment.

"Yes, I do," Malcolm said. "We were considering signing her to our label."

"Have you met with her in person?" Eddie said.

"I have," Malcolm said. "I was down in Austin a few months ago to meet with her and see if she was a good fit for Nations Roots."

"A good fit," Eddie said. "Right. Do you know Jacob Lee?"

"Mr. Lee is a former employee," Malcolm said. "He worked with us for several years to identify acts that might be good for our label."

"Former employee?" Eddie said.

"Yes, sadly we had to let him go," Malcolm said. "He was becoming out of touch with the younger music scene and in all honesty was more trouble than he was worth."

"When did this separation occur?" Eddie said.

"I informed him of our decision when I was in Austin to meet with Mari Simon," Malcolm said.

"Are you aware of Ms. Simon having a stalker?" Eddie said.

"No, I'm not," Malcolm said. "You certainly don't think it's Jacob?"

"Do you think it could be?" Eddie said.

"No," Malcolm said. "She isn't his type."

"What's his type?" Eddie said.

"Young boys," Malcolm said. "Another reason we had to let him go."

"I see," Eddie said. "Was he ever arrested?"

"Not that young," Malcolm said. "College-aged. We got a few complaints from students and counselors at the university."

"I really appreciate your time, Mr. Evers," Eddie said. "One more thing. Did Mari Simon rejecting your sexual advances have any effect on your decision whether to sign her to your label?"

The line was quiet.

"Mr. Evers?" Eddie said.

"I have no idea what you're talking about."

"I thought not," Eddie said. "But if I even get a feeling that it did or hear of any other incongruities in your behavior, I'll have my colleagues at the Nashville field office have a look into your business, and perhaps give our friends at the IRS a call."

"I don't appreciate threats, we run a clean business here," Malcolm said.

"That you may, but having two different agencies investigating you sure wouldn't look good to new acts you want to sign," Eddie said. "From now on keep it professional with your clients."

He hung up the phone and watched the boats on Town Lake. Just as he was putting his phone away to leave, it vibrated in his hand. He glanced at the number that appeared and answered.

"Holland."

"Eddie, it's Ben Olson. I got something for you."

"What is it?" Eddie said.

"We've picked up some intel on Aran Driscoll from friends at the Agency," Ben said. "The unofficial word is that Driscoll works for a group out of Geneva."

"So he's not a freelancer?" Eddie said.

"No. He's very well backed and very well paid," Ben said. "This group is thought to be responsible for some of the most high profile assassinations in a dozen countries."

"You have any names? A handler?" Eddie said.

"We're working on it," Ben said. "We've been able to track some of Driscoll's email traffic and the only address he consistently replies to originates in Canada."

"Canada?" Eddie said.

"Yup, in a small town right across the bridge from Detroit," Ben said.

"Do we have anything we can act on, or bring the Mounties in on?" Eddie said.

"Nothing concrete, but we've been talking to them already," Ben said. "They don't like the idea of hit men being run from their side of the border. They're open to working with us, just working through the logistics now."

"Excellent," Eddie said. "Thanks for the head's up, and keep me informed."

"That's not all," Ben said. "We got some information on Declan Driscoll as well. Aran's father worked for the same group."

"His father was a mercenary, too?" Eddie said. "He kept a low profile. We have nothing on him except that he's presumed dead. Any info on where he operated?"

"Middle east, primarily," Ben said. "His hit list was a long one. The Agency believes him dead also, specifically from a drone strike in the Afghan desert."

"You gotta get me into my old files," Eddie said.

"We're already going through them with the new information, but I went up to the top floor and got you access," Ben said. "But only from the van over a secure connection."

"Done," Eddie said.

With Gus recovering in the hospital, he spent all day in the van and evenings and into the night with Gus. He spent the next week staring at the screen in the command van on Research Boulevard.

He'd worked with the electronic files for years at the JTTF but had been out of the bureau too long. It took time to get used to the system again. Hour by hour the reports and missions came back to him. He'd recall a detail about one thing that would remind him of another.

Deep into the fifth day he came across a report that had been filed shortly before his leave of absence. It listed casualties from a drone strike that occurred six months before he'd left on his leave of absence. He cross-referenced the report to find the initial research that lead to the strike. At the bottom of the recommendation for action was his signature.

Many people would have seen, read and signed off on the action report before an actual strike was ordered, but his signature began the process.

In the report it listed 18 dead including three unidentified men, at least one thought not to be from the region. While accessing all the data he found the images taken by the army team that went in to do recovery and verification. Most of the bodies were charred and burned beyond being able to tell who they were, much less their nationality. Three were not as destroyed. Of those, two had the dark olive complexion commonly found in the Middle East. The final one had light skin, pink from being in the harsh desert sun. The skin could be seen only on the left arm, the rest of the body was burned.

Eddie grabbed his phone and dialed.

"Ben, I found something," he said.

CHAPTER 31

"You came back?" the waitress poured fresh coffee for them.

"Couldn't keep us away," Eddie said.

"The owner said to thank you guys for replacing the window," she said. "Pain in the ass to go through insurance."

"Not a problem," Gus said.

"What happened to you, sweetie?" she looked at Gus.

"Walked into a door," Gus said.

The waitress tilted her head and scowled at him.

"Must have been a pretty big door," she said.

Gus had been in the hospital for the better part of a

week before being released. He was still bruised and his hair was growing in slowly but most of the swelling was gone. He was off of the painkillers except for an occasional Tylenol for headaches.

Eddie looked at the wound running down the side of his friend's head.

"Sure you don't want to borrow one of my hats?" Eddie said.

"I'm sure," Gus said. "Wouldn't want anyone mistaking me for you."

The men sat at their usual table in the diner, the new sheet of glass still mostly clean from being installed two weeks earlier. The sun was setting and the long shadows were crawling across the parking lot.

"Not nervous sitting here again?" Eddie said.

Gus looked out the window and down towards the Belvedere Hotel.

"Nah," Gus said. "He's more creative than that, I think."

The black touchscreen phone resting on the table in front of Gus began to vibrate. He picked it up and pressed the button to answer.

"Ramirez."

"Gus, it's Phillips. We just got a call from San Antonio," Agent Phillips said. "The phone we sent up from the bombing has been ringing."

"What?" Gus said.

"They've traced the caller to another burner phone but it keeps shutting off then showing up in a different location around Austin," Phillips said.

"I'm on my way back to the office," Gus said. "Get CART to forward the calls to a new cell in the van with the same number. Make sure all data transfers."

"Will do," Phillips said.

Gus hung up and relayed the information to Eddie.

"What the hell?" Eddie said. "He's trying to call his own phone?"

"I think he's trying to call you," Gus said.

They left the diner and Eddie drove and pushed the speed of Gus's SUV. They pulled up to the van outside the demolished office building eight minutes later. As he stepped into the van a man handed him a cellphone.

"It's all set up and data is intact," Phillips said.

"Thanks," Gus took the phone. "How often has it been ringing?"

"They said at least once an hour," Phillips said. "Hasn't rung since we got it set up."

"So we wait," Gus said.

"I'm not good at waiting," Eddie said.

Eddie took the phone from Gus and went through the

menu to find the last incoming call and pressed to dial the number. It was answered after two rings.

"What took ya so long?" Aran Driscoll's voice came through the earpiece.

"I was getting a mani-pedi," Eddie said. "Didn't want to mess my nails up."

"Always so glib, aren't ya?" Aran said.

The agents in the van were capturing the audio from the call and patched it through the computer. Gus pulled on a pair of headphones to listen.

"While you were off having dinner with your boyfriend, I've been preparing a little game for you," Aran said.

Eddie glanced at Gus as they realized Aran Driscoll had been watching them at the diner.

"What kind of game?" Eddie said.

"How are ya at being in several places at once?" Aran asked.

"Quit the riddles. Let's just end this. Tell me where to be and I'll be there," Eddie said. "I'm ready for you."

"Oh now that's not fun. Let's do it my way. I'm sure your people are tracking me by now so I'll let you figure it out," Aran said. "And you better be quick. Tick. Tock."

The line went dead.

Eddie looked up at the large screen showing the trace

of Aran's phone. The dot that represented the burner phone was over a building southeast of town.

"Get APD on the phone and get them out there," Gus said. "Call SWAT and HRT out of San Antonio and get them mobilized in case we need them."

Eddie turned and pushed through the van door and Gus chased him into the parking lot.

"Let our guys handle this," Gus said.

"You saw where he was, right?" Eddie pulled the door closed on his rental car he'd left there earlier in the day. "Give me your backup."

"What?" Gus said.

"My Glock's at home," Eddie said. "Give me your backup."

"Dammit, Eddie," Gus said. He looked back at the van then to Eddie.

Eddie revved the car engine to prod Gus.

"Turn that rental piece of shit off and get in my car," Gus said. "I have sirens."

Gus climbed into his SUV and Eddie jumped from the Impala and got into the driver's seat. Gus was still on orders not to drive after his concussion. Eddie had the engine started and the large vehicle moving before he'd even closed his door.

"There's a nine in the armrest and I have a shotgun

and a .45 in the back," Gus said.

Gus pressed the button on his phone to call his team in the van.

"It's Ramirez," Gus said when Phillips answered. "Eddie and I are on our way to Driscoll's last known location. Call me if the signal moves."

Gus hung up and flipped the switch for the lights and sirens as they merged onto the highway that leads towards downtown.

Eddie had the Sig Sauer nine millimeter out of the center console. His left knee pressing up on the steering wheel, he glanced down and checked the magazine and pulled the slide back to put a round into the chamber.

"Keep it together, Eddie," Gus said. "We don't know what we're going to find."

The SUV travelled down the shoulder of the road, the speed hitting over 90 miles per hour and outrunning the sound of the siren. Eddie exited south of downtown and took a wide left turn onto a two-lane road with small houses on either side. An Austin police cruiser flew out from a side street heading to the same location, Eddie slammed on his brakes to avoid hitting it then pressed the gas pedal down further.

The police car in front of him turned left into a dimly lit parking lot and Eddie followed then passed the cruiser as it stopped and he slid to a stop just outside the front door of the building. The two men were out of the SUV and Gus had the hatch open and lifted the panel that concealed the weapons stashed underneath. Gus grabbed the .45mm and Eddie took the shotgun.

"A shotgun. Really?" Gus said.

The police were spreading out through the parking lot on orders to maintain a perimeter and wait on SWAT.

Eddie and Gus looked at each other then entered the building, knowing who Driscoll's target was. They made the first left and moved down the hallway, weapons ready but aimed down to avoid panicking the residents. Gus put his back to the wall and his hand on the doorknob for the stairwell. On Eddie's nod he turned the knob and Eddie pushed through the door, cleared his left side then checked behind the door and began to move up the stairs. Gus followed.

They followed the same drill as they went through the door onto the second floor. Some of the residents looked up at them and their weapons and turned and walked away as quickly as they could, others shrugged and continued what they were doing.

They arrived at the door they needed and took places on either side.

"Let me go in first," Gus said.

"No way," Eddie said.

Gus shook his head, grabbed the doorknob and on Eddie's signal turned it and pushed the door as Eddie entered the dimly lit room, shotgun raised to his shoulder, the barrel scanned left then right. He moved further into the room and looked into the small bathroom and pulled back the curtain on the wheelchair accessible shower.

"Clear," Eddie said.

Eddie lowered the shotgun. Gus had come in behind him and moved forward in the small room, his Sig Sauer still raised as Eddie moved to the bed.

"Is he okay?" Gus said.

Eddie sat the shotgun down on the desk and turned to the bed.

"Dad," he shook his father's shoulders as he was lying in his bed. "Dad, wake up."

The elder Holland's eyes opened and looked at the ceiling then his head turned to Eddie with the same vacant look he'd come used to for years now.

"He's alive," Eddie said.

Gus turned the overhead light on and pulled his phone out and dialed Phillips.

"Alert APD that the target is safe," Gus said. "Secure the entire facility and go room to room."

"Look," Eddie said.

Gus lowered the phone and turned to where Eddie was pointing. Words were written in silver marker across the front of the old CRT television.

'GOOD TRY. TICK. TOCK.'

On top of the television sat a flip phone.

"Your dad have a cell?" Gus said.

"Nope," Eddie said. He picked the phone up and checked recent calls and saw the number of the burner phone they'd talked to Aran on.

"Shit," Eddie said. "He dumped the phone."

As he turned to set the phone down it rang in his hand. Eddie motioned to Gus who turned and walked through the door into the hallway and dialed Agent Phillips number on his own phone.

Eddie pressed the button and answered.

"What," Eddie said.

"That was pretty good," Aran Driscoll's voice came through. "Police were there in less than five minutes and you were only a minute behind them."

"To protect and serve," Eddie said. He moved to the window and pulled the shade to the side to look out across the parking lot.

Gus had Phillips on the line in the hallway. "Get a fix on the number that called the phone we just traced to the nursing home."

"Could you repeat that?" Phillips said.

"The phone Driscoll called from that we traced to the nursing home, get a trace on the current incoming call to that number as fast as you can," Gus said.

"Okay, hold on," Phillips said. "I think I got that."

"You don't protect and serve though, Agent Holland," Aran Driscoll said. "You hunt and kill from thousands of miles away."

"Different mission, same idea," Eddie said. "Protecting our people."

Gus motioned to Eddie and gave a thumb's up. Eddie looked at his father, lying in bed watching them. He covered the mouthpiece on the cellphone.

"I'll come back and see you soon, Dad," Eddie said. He turned and followed Gus down the hallway.

"Well I think that's plenty of time for your little FBI friends," Aran said. "See if you have better luck this time."

Driscoll hung up as Eddie and Gus were in a full run through the hallway, down the stairs and out the front door to Gus's SUV.

Gus got to the driver's seat first.

"You're not cleared to drive," Eddie said. "Move over."

"My truck," Gus said. "It's better that I drive this time anyway."

Eddie relented and ran to the other side and climbed in and pulled his seat belt on.

"You have the location?" Eddie said.

Gus had the truck in reverse, the tires spinning as he backed up. The rear of the SUV hit the front of a police car and he slammed the gearshift into drive and sped out of the parking lot.

"They're gonna be pissed at you," Eddie looked out the back window at the officers gathering around the dented cruiser. "So where is he?"

Gus looked at Eddie out of the corner of his eye then back at the road.

"The hospital," Gus said.

CHAPTER 32

Eddie got his cellphone out and tapped Eva's name to dial her number. Gus had the SUV back on the highway to head to the other side of the city to the hospital where she was on duty in the emergency room.

"Anything?" Gus said.

"Voicemail," Eddie said.

"Eva, call me ASAP," Eddie spoke into his phone. "Strike that. If you get this message, find hospital security or any officer that is in the building, get to a safe location then call me. We'll be there in five minutes."

He hung up. "This thing go any faster?"

Gus glanced at the speedometer.

"We're going 110 through town at night," Gus said. "I'm doing the best I can, this thing handles like a cow. And I'm kinda seeing double right now."

"And this is why you shouldn't be driving with a concussion."

Gus's phone rang and he answered through the hands free on the steering wheel.

"Ramirez," he said.

"We have APD on the way to the hospital," Phillips said. "They already have a couple officers there with a prisoner they had to bring over from county lockup."

"We need to get the hospital locked down and the officers have to locate Dr. Eva Taylor," Gus said. "She's the target."

"Got it," Phillips said.

"Is Driscoll's phone still pinging from the hospital?" Eddie said.

"Yes sir, it is," Phillips said. "It's moving all through the building."

"Thanks," Eddie said. Gus hung up the call.

"He's looking for her," Eddie said.

The SUV slowed as Gus turned the final corner then accelerated on the long drive that lead to the emergency room doors. The men ran from the truck through the sliding doors, guns down to their sides. Eddie left the shotgun in the SUV and had the nine-millimeter Sig.

Staff members recognized Eddie as they all took steps back to move out of their way when they saw the men's guns out.

"Eddie," a nurse called to him.

He turned her direction and she pointed to the curtain at the end of the row of beds in the ER. He nodded to her, raised the pistol and Gus fell in beside him. They moved through the room, scanning their perimeters until they got to the curtain.

Eddie reached and put his hand on the curtain, looked at Gus, then pulled it back. The men stepped forward, guns raised, into the small area.

Eva looked up, her gloved hands bloody while she threaded stitches through the lower lip of a college aged boy.

"What the hell, Eddie?" she said.

Eddie lowered his weapon. Gus turned and stepped away and dialed his phone.

"You're okay?" Eddie said.

"Of course I'm okay," Eva said. "Unfortunately I think Skippy here just shit his pants, but other than that…"

Eddie looked at the boy.

"Your name really Skippy?" Eddie said.

The boy nodded his head.

"Tough break for you," Eddie said.

"We need a full search of the hospital," Gus said into his phone. "Get all APD here that you can. The target is secure."

Gus saw two uniformed officers walk into the emergency room. He walked up to them with his badge raised.

"We know who you are, Gus," the taller officer said.

"Sorry, habit," Gus said. "Give me your radio."

The officer pulled the radio off his belt and unclipped the mic from his shoulder and handed it to Gus.

"Who's running the show?" Gus said.

"Weston," the officer said.

"Thanks," Gus turned and pushed the button on the microphone. "Weston, this is Ramirez."

"I have two Ramirez's on duty, can you be more specific," Weston's voice came through the speaker.

"This is Special Agent Gus Ramirez with the FBI," Gus said. "Is that better?"

"Gus, what do you need?" Weston said. "I have six more units on the way and I'm five minutes out."

"Who do you have here now," Gus said.

"Colson and Hernandez," Weston said. "Which I'm gathering you just took one of their radios. And about an hour ago we sent Kincaid and Ward over from county lockup with a sick prisoner."

Gus looked around the emergency room.

"I don't see them in the ER," Gus said.

"Have to be there somewhere," Weston said. "The prisoner kept complaining of migraines, then passed out on the way back to lockup from dinner, flopping around on the ground like an asshole. Nobody believed him."

Gus turned to Eva.

"Did a prisoner from county come in?" Gus said.

"Forty minutes ago, maybe," Eva said. "Had two officers with him."

"Where is he?" Gus said.

"Went up for an MRI at least twenty or thirty minutes ago," Eva said.

Gus spoke into the phone again. "Weston, what's the prisoner's name?"

"Let me see," the radio crackled as Weston kept the button pressed as he flipped through papers while being driven to the hospital. "Pierce. Adrian Pierce. Hey, isn't that the kid Eddie stopped from killing all those kids at the school a while back?"

Gus turned to the officers. "Keep her safe and lock the ER down. Send any other uniforms and agents that get here to MRI."

Eddie and Gus turned and left the emergency room.

"I'll take the elevator, you take the stairs," Gus said.

They went opposite directions in the hallway. The MRI room was midway down the hall two floors above, between the elevator and the stairwell. Gus stood in the back corner of the large elevator, gun in front of him. Eddie moved up the stairs, aiming above him and watching the hidden corners made by the opening between the flights of stairs. He came out of the stairs and brought his weapon up until he saw Gus step out of the elevator. They moved towards each other, backs to the wall, until they reached the windowless steel door to the MRI facility.

"Rock, paper or scissors?" Gus said.

"Gun," Eddie said. He pushed forward through the heavy door and Gus followed.

They moved into the small vestibule that contained two doors, one on the left that lead to the control room and one straight ahead that went in to the large magnetic resonance imaging machine. The lights were off in both rooms. Eddie motioned with his left hand to cover him as he checked the first room. Gus took his position to see into the control room while watching the darkened room with the machine as well.

With his left hand Eddie turned the knob, his right

hand still aiming his weapon ahead of him. As the door swung open he reached under his gun arm and found the light switch and flipped it to the up position.

"I have one officer on the floor," Eddie said. "Clear."

Eddie stepped back into the small entryway and the two men went to the door to the main room. Gus took lead while Eddie covered him. The door swung in, Gus stepped in and to the left and Eddie followed and went right. Gus found the light switch and the room lit up.

"I have the other officer," Gus said.

Eddie moved around behind the MRI machine then turned to the belt that carried patients into the small opening to be scanned.

"We have feet," Eddie said.

Gus turned with his gun still raised. A pair of bare feet was visible at the end of the tunnel, a green hospital cloth covering the body from the ankles up and into the machine.

"Adrian Pierce?" Eddie said. "That you?"

"Yeah," Adrian said. "Who is that? Who's there?"

"Adrian, this is Eddie Holland. Do you remember me?"

"I do," Adrian said. "You're the asshole who shot at me. I didn't want to help him."

"Help who?" Eddie said.

"The Irish guy," Adrian said. "He told me you'd come."

"How long ago did he leave?" Gus said.

"I don't know. Feels like a long time I've been in here," Adrian said. "But he visited me at the jail. He told me what to do, how to fake being sick to get brought to the hospital. He said he wanted my help to kill you. But I don't want to die."

"Okay, I'm going to bring you out of there," Eddie said.

He reached up to flip the switch to slide the patient out.

"Stop," Gus said.

"What?" Eddie said.

"Remember who we're dealing with here," Gus said.

Eddie looked at Gus then back at the feet.

"You think he's booby trapped?" Eddie said.

"I'd rather know before we start moving him," Gus said.

The door to the room opened behind him as Weston and three other officers stepped in.

"We haven't checked your guys yet," Gus said. "Check for pulses and get them out of here if you can."

"Did the Irish man do anything to you?" Eddie said.

"He taped stuff all over my chest," Adrian said. "It's really heavy."

"I'm going to take a look, try not to move too much."

Eddie knelt beside the belt and peered into the dark tunnel. He lifted the end of the green cloth and let it down.

"You see anything?" Gus said.

"More than I wanted," Eddie said. "He's not wearing underwear."

"Good to know," Gus said. "What about a device?"

"I think calling what I saw a device would be generous, at best," Eddie said.

"Get serious," Gus said.

"I need some light," Eddie turned to the officer in charge. "Weston, got your flashlight on you?"

The police captain pulled the light off of his belt and handed it to Eddie. He turned it on and pointed it into the tunnel.

"I can see the outline of his body under the cloth. It looks bumpy," Eddie said. "I'm taking a look under the cloth again."

"Enjoy the view," Gus said.

Eddie lifted the end of the cloth and pointed the flashlight under the green material. He reached in with the flashlight to raise the cloth more then froze.

"He's wired," Eddie said.

CHAPTER 33

"**L**ooks like it's contained under the blanket, but I couldn't be sure," Eddie said.

Sergeant Buckholtz nodded. "We'll take it from here."

He turned to another bomb squad officer next to him and began to give the orders to remove the explosives.

"Get Levi to bring in the laparoscopic cameras and monitors," Buckholtz said. "I want protective barriers put up on all four walls of the room and on the floor under the machine and over the top. I want to minimize damage if the device blows."

"Anything we can do to help," Gus said.

Buckholtz turned to Gus and Eddie.

"Yeah," he said. "Evacuate the hospital."

Eddie and Gus left the MRI room and found Captain Weston standing with another man in the hallway.

"Gus, this is Frank," Weston said. "Head of hospital security."

"Good to meet you," Gus said. "We need to evacuate."

"The whole building?" Frank said.

"Yes," Gus said. "Do you have an emergency evacuation plan on file?"

"I'll have it pulled up, but I know it," Frank pulled his walkie-talkie from his belt. "Jane, we need the evac plan pulled up and put in action."

"Really?" Jane's voice came through the small speaker.

"Yes, really, and immediately," Frank said. "This is not a drill."

"What can we do?" Eddie said.

"Any second the emergency alarm will sound," Frank said. "Staff knows what to do. First thing is to make sure no surgeries start and then to see where others are in their progress. There's a chance an operating room will have to stay occupied if they can't stop where they are. I'm going to head there now. You two help where you can, but everyone knows what to do and you might just get in the way. All available ambulances in the county will be called to get here to load up critical patients first. Non critical patients can walk or be wheeled out and wait for a truck to come back and get them."

"Ever done this before?" Eddie said.

"Not a real one," Frank said. "But I've read that manual at least a hundred times and we do a full drill once a year."

A soft pinging tone began to play through the halls from the overhead speakers.

"That the alarm?" Eddie said. "It's not very alarming."

"Yeah, it's designed to not panic patients and to keep staff calm, too," Frank said.

Eddie and Gus headed to the stairs and down to the ER. Nurses were already packing supplies into bags and getting mobile patients moving to the door. The first ambulance showed up a minute later from the fire station across the street and sirens could be heard as more were on their way down the street.

Eva was directing traffic and triaging patients for exit from the building. Patients began to start flowing through from the elevators and stairs from the rooms above, accompanied by doctors, nurses, kitchen workers and any other staff that could help. More ambulances arrived and loaded the patients that needed the most attention, fitting two and three in the back of each truck.

Gus pulled his phone out and dialed. "Phillips, any update on the last trace?"

"It went dark a few minutes ago," Phillips said.

"Okay, let me know if it changes," Gus said.

Eddie was watching the hospital staff move patients and equipment out of the hospital.

"They really have this down," Eddie said.

"They sure do," Gus said. "You thinking what I am?"

"Go get a drink?" Eddie said.

"No," Gus said. "Driscoll might be watching."

"If he is he'll see us come out," Eddie said.

"What do you want to do?" Gus said.

Eddie looked around at the shelves of supplies.

"I'm walking out the door. Once I'm at a distance I'll circle back and check the perimeter," Eddie said.

"How are you going to walk out the door without him seeing you?" Gus said.

Eddie grabbed a green hospital gown from a cart beside one of the emergency room beds and pulled it on over his clothes. He took his hat off and hung a blanket over his head.

"Really?" Gus said.

"Really," Eddie said.

An ambulance was about to close its back doors to

transport two patients to the university hospital a few miles away. Eddie sat down in a wheelchair that was coming back in through the door and asked the nurse to roll him out to the ambulance. They caught the paramedic and Eddie climbed into the back of the truck, the door closed and the unit pulled away.

"Who are you?" the paramedic said.

"Just hitching a ride," Eddie said. He pulled the gown off and put his hat back on. "Just drop me off about half a mile down the road."

"Sure," the paramedic yelled up to the driver to stop at the end of the street and let Eddie out.

Eddie set out at a jog and cut through a neighborhood to avoid the main road. It was dark out now and he moved slower than he could to keep from tripping. He jumped a chain link fence into the tree line that surrounded the hospital grounds. From there he moved behind the overgrowth watching for anybody hiding in the woods.

As he moved he watched through the trees to the hospital then stopped. The ground had elevated no more than a few feet but it created a clear sightline from the trees to the emergency room door. He moved forward through the trees until he reached that last big oak before the field opened up in front of him, beyond it the helipad and the emergency room.

He looked down and stepped around the tree. On the ground was a grey cellphone.

"Son of a bitch," Eddie said.

He picked up the phone and flipped it open. He checked the settings to find it was the same one they'd traced to the hospital. He pulled his phone out and dialed.

"Gus," Eddie said. "I got the phone."

He filled Gus in on his search through the trees.

"EOD is clear," Gus said. "Pierce was wired up good, but it was a simple device. They're hauling it away now to destroy it."

"Pierce okay?" Eddie said.

"A bit rattled, but he'll live," Gus said.

"Good, they can get him back to jail and get him locked up for a long time," Eddie said.

"They've cancelled the evac and they're bringing all the patients back. The police chief is walking in now. I'm going to be here a while," Gus said. "Take my car, I'll get a ride later."

CHAPTER 34

"How long've you been singin'?" Aran said. He sat across from the young woman and listened to her talk and stared at the line of her neck as it dove down into her blouse, his mind momentarily becoming lost in the penumbra where shadows and light dance.

"My whole life but mostly when I was alone. I didn't sing in front of an audience until a high school talent show, then I was hooked," Mari said.

The restaurant's lights were low and candles at each table illuminated the faces of the guests with moving shadows and an orange glow.

"I started performing a couple years ago on my own then put my band together," Mari said. "That's when things really picked up for me. I'd always thought of myself as a solo act, a singer songwriter type, but being in front of a group of incredible musicians pushes you somewhere new."

"So I can say 'I knew you when' after you're a big famous celebrity," Aran said.

Mari smiled and tilted her head.

"That you might," she said. "Enough about me. What part of Ireland are you from?"

He was crossing the line he had vowed not to cross, bringing a civilian into his world. The wine, low lights and the beauty of the woman across from him were conflicting with fifteen years of solitude.

"Belfast," he said.

She sipped her wine and gently nodded her head.

"Did you know anyone involved with the IRA?" she said.

He locked eyes with her and saw a life different than the one he'd been living, one where he could share instead of having one-night stands or rough nights with prostitutes who reeked of cigarette smoke.

"I was. So was my Da," he said. His voice turned cold and his gaze went to the room around them, making sure no one else was hearing their conversation.

He had said so much more than he had to anyone. But as much as he looked at her and wished he could have her, he knew her fate. His secrets wouldn't go very far.

Mari sat back in her chair.

"Wow. Sorry. I didn't mean to pry," she said.

"It's fine. I don't talk about it much, seems like two lifetimes ago," he said.

"How do you go on after that?" she said.

He picked up the bottle of wine and swirled it to see how much was left then poured a little into his glass and the rest into hers.

"My Da and I were walking in the woods one day. It was warm, but we wore long coats to cover the weapons we always carried," Aran said. "We were talking about just that. The cease-fire was about to be signed that would end the Troubles for good. Neither of us had any experience other than fighting. He told me he'd been talking to a man who needed men like us and with our war about to end, the only choice we had was to find a new one."

Mari had lifted her glass then set it back down without drinking. He watched her eyes to see where she was and what was going to happen. The plan was to leave the restaurant quietly. The small envelope filled with white powder was in his pocket in case he needed to get it into her drink.

Her posture softened and she picked her glass up again.

"So what is it you do for a living now?" she said.

"Ahh, well," Aran drank the last of his wine. "I'm a world traveler. I take care of things other people don't want to take care of."

"What kinds of things?" Mari said.

"Messy things," Aran said.

"Ooh, sounds ominous," Mari said. "Should I be scared of you?"

"Yes," Aran said.

Mari laughed and brought her glass to her mouth. Aran laughed with her, his eyes watching her lips move as she sipped her wine.

CHAPTER 35

T he SUV rolled through downtown on the way back to Eddie's apartment. He considered stopping for a beer but decided against it while driving an FBI vehicle. The radio was on a news station and he pressed the buttons until he found KGSR. Arc Angel's "Living in a Dream" came on and he turned it up as he came to a stop at a red light and he sang along. His phone beeped and he pulled it out of his pocket to read the message.

"I have something you may want. Come alone."

Another beep and a photo filled the small screen, the image of Mari Simon on her knees, duct tape holding her mouth shut and hands tied behind her back.

Eddie tapped the screen to enlarge the photograph and scrolled around the image to see the wooden floors and just on the left edge of the frame was the leg of a barstool.

"Buddy's," Eddie said.

He checked his mirror and pulled a U-turn then dialed his phone, put it on speaker and dropped it on the seat beside him. He flipped a switch on the dashboard.

"What's up?" Gus answered. "Are you using my siren?"

"Driscoll has Mari," Eddie said. "They're at Buddy's. I'm two minutes out."

"I'll get my guys and APD on the way," Gus said. "Dammit, HRT just headed back to San Antonio."

"The hostage rescue team won't do any good," Eddie said. "I don't think he intends for this to be a drawn out process."

"I'm guessing you won't wait for us before going in," Gus said.

"That's a pretty good guess," Eddie said. "Just get me some backup on the way. And an ambulance."

"There's no way I'm letting you get this asshole alone," Gus said.

The line went dead.

He parked a block from Buddy's Music Saloon and

went to the back of the SUV and found an extra magazine for the Sig. He paused to think about bringing the shotgun but decided against it with Mari in the crossfire.

"Really wish I had my Glock," he said.

He walked close to the buildings on the same side of the street as the club. The bar had no windows and the glass on the recessed front door was blacked out. Eddie chose not to bottleneck himself in the narrow entry and moved around behind the building. The back door had been pried open and was not closed all the way.

"This is pretty stupid, Eddie," he said.

He held the pistol in his right hand as he opened the door and stepped into the dark backroom of the bar. He held the door as it closed to avoid making a sound. It was too dark in the room to see. He moved through the backroom, avoiding cases and kegs of beer, to get to the door that opened into the main bar.

He pushed the swinging door and opened it an inch to look through. He could see only shadows moving. He couldn't go any further without making noise.

"It's Eddie Holland," he said. "I'm alone."

He heard Mari Simon's muffled voice as she struggled to scream through the duct tape.

"You made it," Aran said. "Don't be shy, come on out

and play with us. I'm sure you have your gun, but so do I so it's a fun little party."

Eddie pushed through the door and let it swing back, not concerned about the noise anymore. His gun still raised, finger stretched out across the trigger guard, he moved from the shadows behind the stage into the main room of the bar.

Mari Simon was on her knees in the middle of the stage wearing jeans and a black tank top, a single light shined down on her, hair covered her face. Blood was on her bare shoulders and arms. He moved towards the stage.

"No, no, not so quickly," Aran Driscoll's voice came from the darkness behind him.

Eddie turned away from the stage and scanned the rest of the room.

"So, Aran," Eddie said. "Is it time to have our little talk?"

"What would you like to talk about?" Aran said.

"Oh, I don't know. Maybe why you've made it your life's mission to destroy me," Eddie said.

"Ahh, that little thing," Aran said. "I'd have thought you'd want to talk about your friend Mari first, the whole 'let her go and I'll stay' bit."

"That'll come," Eddie said. "I thought I'd ease into it."

"Then why don't you put that gun away and we can just have a nice little talk," Aran said.

Eddie stepped into the middle of the floor and then saw Aran Driscoll, sitting on a bar stool in the shadows of the far corner. He had no gun in his hands. Eddie set the Sig Sauer on top of a tall bar table in front of the stage and stepped away from it.

"So?" Eddie said.

"It saddens me we've made it this far and you don't know why I'm here," Aran said. "You managed to find out who I am, but that's it."

"You've done a good job of hiding your past," Eddie said. "But mercenaries generally do."

"Oh how I hate that word," Aran said. "My father preferred 'consultant.' I just say 'killer.'"

"Your father approved of what you do?" Eddie said.

"He taught me everything I know."

"So after the fighting stopped in Ireland, you became consultants, killers, whatever you want to call yourself. I'm thinking you worked mainly in Europe and America but your father had a taste for the exotic."

"You've been doing your research," Aran said. "Is that all you've got?"

"He liked the middle east," Eddie said. "After years of the Irish rain and cold he built up a taste for the desert.

Is that about right?"

"Who do you think helped teach Al-Qaeda to build those IED's?" Aran said. "Iraq, Afghanistan, Pakistan. He even had some good friends in Dubai. Oh, how he loved Dubai."

"Unless you want a good drink," Eddie said.

"The people he worked with got the best liquor. Not the watered down shite from the hotel bars," Aran said. "And they also funded him really well. Then one day he was working on the Afghan border when a huge feckin' bomb was dropped on him with U.S.A. written down the side of it."

"And you think I did it?" Eddie said.

"I know you did," Aran said.

"I sat behind a desk in Virginia," Eddie said. "I did research and wrote reports on where we thought the terrorists were operating."

"You are so modest, Mr. Holland," Aran said. "I know you were with the Joint Terrorism Task Force and I know you made detailed plans for your fighter pilots and drones to drop bombs."

"I didn't drop the bombs," Eddie said.

"Now that's just sad, Eddie. Trying to pass the blame on to the military?" Aran said. "You may not have pushed the buttons, but they were pushed because you said they should be."

"We were at war with them," Eddie said. "It wasn't your dad's war. He chose to be there."

The front door of the bar swung open.

"Who the hell is in my bar," Buddy Bowen walked in, baseball bat in his hand. He saw Mari on the stage, hands behind her and duct tape across her mouth.

"Mari! What the fuck is going?" Buddy moved towards her.

"Get out, Buddy," Eddie said. "Just run."

A pistol appeared in Aran's hand and three shots were fired, hitting Buddy in the back as he was going for the stage. Eddie turned and began to make the few quick steps back to the table where his gun sat waiting.

"Stop," Aran said. "You can leave it there."

Eddie froze, his fingers inches from his weapon. He spent a few moments calculating if he could pick it up and fire before Aran could get a round off and decided he couldn't. If it were someone unseasoned, not as comfortable with the weapon, perhaps he'd try. But Aran Driscoll was a trained killer.

"Is this really how we want it to end between you and me?" Aran said. "I could shoot you, but then you'd be dead or you might get to your gun and shoot me before you die... and it would be over. Where's the fun in that?"

"What are you suggesting?" Eddie said. His hand was still reaching towards the gun.

Aran raised his left hand in the air then squatted and placed his gun on the floor. He stood then kicked it away.

"Don't you want to hurt me?" Aran said.

"Since you mention it, I have had a few very vivid dreams about breaking your nose with my fist," Eddie said.

"That's what I'm talking about," Aran said. "Mano a mano."

Eddie took his porkpie hat off and sat it beside the Sig Sauer nine millimeter and stepped away from the table and out into the middle of the barroom floor.

"You prepared to meet your god?" Aran said.

"I don't have a god," Eddie said.

"An atheist in Texas? I didn't think that was possible," Aran said. "I thought you all thumped your bibles and relied on the man upstairs to guide you."

"Not everyone," Eddie said. "And didn't you fight for your religion for years? Killing other men because they didn't think the way you think."

"It wasn't that they didn't think the same. It was that they wanted to tell me how I could think, what I could believe," Aran said.

"Sounds like we have something in common then," Eddie said. "I hate being told what to do."

Aran moved towards him, hands down but loose, ready to strike. The Irishman had an inch in height over Eddie and a slight advantage on arm length, as well as the experience of having killed many people with his hands. Eddie sized him up and prepared to keep a steady distance.

Aran lunged forward. His right hand flew out as his shoulder rotated into the punch and struck Eddie in the chest, a rib cracked.

Eddie stumbled back. With a quick double step Aran moved in to strike again. Eddie took a fast step and closed the distance faster than his opponent expected and reduced the impact of the punch. His right hand came up and landed on Aran's nose with the added momentum of the two men moving towards each other.

The sound of his cartilage shattering stopped Aran before he even felt the pain from the broken nose. Blood covered his mouth and chin and he wiped it away with his hand.

"Very good," Aran said. "Got that out of the way early."

Aran threw a left hook that caught Eddie's jaw and continued the combination with a straight right to the face then a left uppercut to the rib that had just been broken, doubling him over.

Still bent over, Eddie strained to catch his breath. With no eyes on him Aran pulled a six-inch knife from the backside of his leather belt. He ran forward as Eddie straightened up, the knife held with the blade running up the inside of his forearm. He swung a wide left, the blade came out of the bottom of his fist at Eddie's face. The tip of the sharp edge caught Eddie's cheek as he leaned back to avoid being cut. Eddie leaned back in after the arm passed him and with his left arm pushed Aran past him and took a step away.

"So much for mano a mano?" Eddie said.

"I never said I played fair," Aran said.

The men circled each other. The blade of Aran's knife stayed hidden, concealing where it might strike next. Eddie feinted a right towards Aran's face to get a reaction. Aran took the bait and stepped right and moved in towards Eddie, the knife coming out with a tight swing towards Eddie's head again. Anticipating the move, Eddie ducked below the knife hand as it travelled over his head and brought his right hand up into Aran's ribs as his opponent's back turned to him. As the Irishman began to double over, Eddie reached and took the knife hand in his right and pushed Driscoll's head left with other hand, stretching the man's right arm. His knee came up and through the elbow. The joint gave and Eddie felt the limb go limp.

Aran fell to his knees and the knife dropped to the floor, the arm muscle no longer able to grip the handle. Eddie kicked the blade across the room then stepped to Aran and brought his foot up into the Irishman's ribs. Blood sprayed from the man's mouth as he flipped onto his back on the wooden floor. Eddie covered the distance to the Sig and turned as Aran began to sit up and reached for his pistol he had kicked away earlier. Eddie pulled the trigger, a single round struck the right shoulder blade, tearing through muscle and bone and Aran collapsed again.

Eddie stepped to Buddy's body and checked for a pulse but found none. Sirens could be heard as they came down 6th street towards the bar from two directions. He went to the edge of the stage and lifted Mari and turned and sat her on a chair.

"Get ready, fast is the only way to do this," Eddie said. She nodded and he pulled the duct tape from her mouth in one motion then began to remove the tape from her wrists.

"Are you okay?" he said. "You need to run. Get outside. The police are pulling up now."

Mari fell into Eddie's body and she wrapped her arms around him, almost sending him backwards into the stage. He stood, pulling her up with him. He heard a boot scuff on the floor and looked over Mari's shoulder towards Aran Driscoll.

The first bullet hit Mari in the middle of her back and passed between her ribs and through her left lung then exited her body and entered Eddie's chest. Aran pulled the trigger again as Eddie turned to block Mari and felt the projectile go into his right side below his raised arm as it shielded her. Aran climbed to his feet, a small two shot .22-caliber pistol in his left hand that had been hidden in a holster under the leg of his jeans. The sounds of sirens became louder as the first vehicles began to pull up outside.

Eddie held Mari's body as she struggled to breathe, blood mixed with fluid from her left lung bubbled out through the hole in her chest onto Eddie as his own blood streamed out of the bullet wounds in his chest and side. He looked up to see Aran Driscoll stumble out of view behind the stage then heard the back door slam closed.

CHAPTER 36

E ddie was rolled into the emergency room on the cot from the ambulance. The paramedics had cut his blood soaked shirt away and placed four-by-four gauze pads over the gunshot wounds to slow the bleeding on the way to the hospital. The ER nurses took over and started to clean around the wounds to evaluate the damage. Eva came in and looked at the small hole in his chest.

"Hey there," Eddie said.

"Really?" Eva said. "Hey there? You've been shot. Twice."

"Most of the blood is Mari's," Eddie said.

"You're impossible, Eddie," Eva said. She pulled back the gauze and began to inspect the injuries and found the small projectile just below the surface in his chest. Passing through Mari's body it had slowed down enough to not go too far into him. She lifted his right arm and he groaned as she looked for the source of the blood.

"We have one just under the skin in his chest and another appears to have bounced off of a rib on his right side," Eva said. "Call up and get a room ready for surgery immediately, we're sending him straight up."

Gus came running up to the bed.

"Where's Driscoll?" Eddie said. The bed he had been transferred to began to roll towards the elevator.

"Gone. He's just gone," Gus said. "We couldn't have missed him by more than a minute or two. Every car possible is on the road looking for him."

Eddie looked at the ceiling. The events of the hours that led up to this moment ran through his head. A needle went into his arm and an IV was set up to replace blood and fluids in his body and relax him.

"He's hurt bad," Eddie said. "Can't get far. He'll need medical help."

"We're looking for him, Eddie," Gus said.

"Where's Mari?" Eddie said.

"She's in surgery," Eva said. "She got here five

minutes before you and they took her straight up."

"Buddy's dead," Eddie said.

"There was nothing we could do," Eva said.

"We have to find him, Gus," Eddie said.

"I know," Gus said. "I have everyone on it."

Eddie faded to sleep as the drugs injected into the IV began to take control of him. Gus and Eva stepped back and watched the elevator door close in front of them.

CHAPTER 37

The first day in the hospital Eddie mostly slept. Whenever he woke up he began to take sensors off of his skin and one time even got the IV out of his arm before the nurses were in his room and had him sedated again. By the second day he'd given up trying to escape and accepted the fact that his body had to heal before he could go after Aran Driscoll.

In the hours he couldn't move and when he should be sleeping, he stared at the ceiling. Thoughts of Buddy Bowen lying on the floor of his bar, Mari Simon shot through the chest and his best friend put in the hospital kept running through his head. And he had put his sister's family in danger for a second time.

Just as Eddie had done, Gus sat vigil with his best friend. He had his team working on every lead while he worked the phones from Eddie's bedside. He was still recovering from the concussion Aran Driscoll had given him.

"Anything?" Eddie said.

He was on his feet and preparing for a walk down the hall on his third day when Gus walked in. The combination of the broken rib and the gunshot wounds had set him back further then either would have alone, but he was pushing his recovery.

"Not yet," Gus said. "We've got all the borders under watch and alerts with the airlines. Every hospital within six states has a BOLO, including border towns in Mexico."

"He's spent the last fifteen years off the radar," Eddie said. "If he doesn't want to be found, he won't be."

"We'll find him," Gus said. "It may take a while, but we'll find him. He's not used to having people who actually know his name. He'll slip up, and we'll be watching."

"I hope you're right," Eddie said.

"You know I am," Gus said. "I have calls in to some contacts at Langley, too."

"What about overseas?" Eddie said.

"It's handled. Everyone who can possibly help has been contacted," Gus said.

CHAPTER 38

The funeral for Buddy Bowen was small and quiet. The party that followed was anything but. The doors to Buddy's Music Saloon were closed to the general public, but since almost everyone along 6th Street knew him, the bar was packed. A long list of local bands had volunteered to play and the music went into the night. Ian Moore was on stage singing a soulful rendition of his song "Today" with only his electric guitar and a drummer behind him, the slow soulful dirge drawing everyone's attention.

Eddie sat in a chair by the wall, his chest bound with tape to protect the broken rib. The bullet wounds were stitched and healing. Eva sat beside him on the bench seat and Gus and Shelley were across from them. They all held shot glasses and downed the brown liquid and slammed the glasses back onto the bar.

"Okay, party boy," Eva said. "I'm cutting you off. You're still on pain killers."

"I threw them away yesterday," Eddie said. "I kept thinking my phone was ringing when it wasn't."

"It's only been a week," Eva said. "Don't try to be tough."

"I'm fine. Plus, a couple more of these shots and I won't be feeling anything," Eddie said. "I might even be up for some fun when we get home."

"Eww. Big sister. Sitting right here," Shelley said.

"So how was Florida?" Gus said.

"Disgusting, expensive, hot, humid," Shelley said. "But the kids loved it."

Eddie motioned to the bar and a waitress brought another tray of shots. The owners of several other clubs came on stage and were sharing stories about Buddy. As they finished everyone raised a glass in the air then drank to their friend.

"You all knew him a long time," Eva said.

"We did indeed," Gus said. "Eddie was closer to him because to football, but we all spent time together."

"I was two years ahead of Buddy and had a crush on him most of my senior year," Shelley said. "But it would have been social suicide to date a sophomore so I never let him know."

"He knew," Eddie said.

"What?" Shelley said. "I'm so retroactively embarrassed now."

"He always loved music," Eddie said. "When everyone was talking about college or military, Buddy was talking about this. About owning his own bar."

They looked around at the crowd that had gathered, people smiling and talking about Buddy Bowen. Another band that had gotten its start at the bar was setting up to play a few songs. Eddie wished Mari was well enough to be here. He turned to his friends and raised his glass.

"I'm buying it," Eddie said.

"It's open bar," Shelley said. "All the other clubs pitched in to cover the cost tonight."

"No, I'm buying the bar," Eddie said.

"You're drunk," Eva said.

"Maybe," Eddie said. "But I'm buying the bar."

Everyone looked around at each other then at Eddie.

"What are you talking about?" Eva said.

"I talked with Buddy's sister earlier today," he said.

"She a lawyer in Houston. Their parents are in a retirement village near Corpus Christi. None of them want the bar."

"You're serious?" Gus said.

"Yup," Eddie said. "Buddy paid the mortgage off on the space a few years ago and was actually in the black. He wasn't getting rich, but he always seemed happy."

"What about the Bureau?" Gus said.

"We all know I was never going back full time," Eddie said. "I can still consult. Buddy only worked late a couple nights a week. He has a great staff here. And look at me. I can't play cops and robbers the rest of my life."

"You're buying a bar," Gus said.

"I'm buying a bar," Eddie said.

"I want in," Gus said.

"What, you want to go in with me?"

"Yes, I do," Gus said.

"But you just heard about this 30 seconds ago and you want in?" Eddie said.

"Definitely," Gus said. "But isn't there someone you should discuss this with first?"

"You're right," Eddie looked at his sister. "Shelley, what do you think about me buying the bar?"

Eva rolled her eyes. "I would punch you in the ribs right now if I didn't know how much it would actually hurt you."

Eddie turned in his seat to face Eva.

"Whaddya think?" he said.

Eva looked at Eddie and ran her hands down the sides of his face.

"I can't think of a more ridiculous, wonderful idea," she said.

CHAPTER 39

The broken rib proved to be more difficult for Eddie than the bullet wounds. Skin healed and the soreness faded, but the rib kept Eddie from running or doing almost anything that exerted more energy than being still.

He'd spent the days leading up to Buddy's wake sitting in a chair at Eva's house staring at the television as he constantly changed channels. After the party he began moving around more with short walks outside. A week later he was spending time at the bar during the day, working on the paperwork to close the purchase to him and Gus and to get to know his new staff and see how Buddy had run the business.

Mari Simon recovered more slowly than Eddie. The bullet had torn a hole in one of her lungs. It was a month after the fight in the bar when she walked back through the doors, her Uncle Dom at her side.

"I heard you took over here," she said.

Eddie looked up and smiled.

"Mari, it's so good to see you," he gave her a gentle hug. "I came by your room a couple of times at the hospital but you were always sleeping then I heard you were transferred up to Dallas."

"You sure I wasn't just pretending to sleep to avoid you?" she said.

"I wouldn't blame you," Eddie said. "I can't tell you how sorry I am that you got pulled into that."

"It'll make a great song someday," she said. "They ever catch the guy?"

"Not yet, but we're still looking," Eddie said. "Men like that who don't want to be found are pretty good at staying hidden."

"Well, I hope you do," Mari said.

"And Dom, I'm sure you're regretting ever calling me," Eddie said.

"Never," the priest said. "The man above has a reason for everything."

"Right," Eddie said and nodded.

"This time he's right," Mari said. "I got a call two weeks ago from a label in New York. They'd heard about the shooting and finally gave my demos a listen."

"And?" Eddie said.

"Well, the lawyers are going over it now, but looks like I have a record deal," she said.

"That's so great," Eddie said. "But now you'll be too big to play here again."

"This is my home stage, if you'll still have me," Mari said.

"You just tell me when you're ready and the stage is yours," Eddie said.

"Deal," Mari said.

"So, I'm glad you're both here," Eddie said. "I need to show you something."

Eddie walked past the stage and into the backroom and Dom and Mari followed. He opened to door to the office and sat down at the desk and rolled the computer mouse back and forth to get the old PC to wake up. The screen came to life and Eddie clicked through a few folders.

"I was digging around Buddy's files that didn't look work related to see if there was anything I needed to share with his family," Eddie said. "When I found this."

Deep in a subfolder of the computers operating system was a folder simply called 'iram'. Eddie double clicked the folder and it opened on the screen to show more than a hundred photographs of Mari Simon.

"Oh my god," Mari said. "It was Buddy all that time?"

"Looks that way," Eddie said. "I knew the man since elementary school and never would have guessed it. I should have known, should have seen it. But when you're too close to something it's too hard to see."

"At least we know, I guess," Mari said. "Feels weird. He was a good friend, I thought. And the whole time he was…"

"Obsessing?" Eddie said.

"Yeah," Mari said. "He was at those private events and shows in other cities and I never saw him."

"I cross checked those dates with the club, and either there was no show here those nights or he'd left his bartender in charge," Eddie said. "He probably just hung back in the crowds to make sure you didn't see him."

"Thank you for showing us, Eddie," Dom said. "It isn't quite the closure we'll have when you catch the man who shot the two of you, but it at least ends one chapter."

"And when we get the guy, you'll be two of the first to know," Eddie said.

"Sounds good," Mari said. "And, thank you. For everything."

"You're welcome," Eddie said.

"Your girlfriend is very lucky to have a man like you," she put her arms around him and lay her head down on his shoulder. He held her as tightly as was comfortable until she released him.

"Mind if I have a minute with your uncle?" he said.

"Sure, I'll go catch up with the others," Eva turned and left the small office.

"What did you want to talk about?" Dom said.

"Well, I was wondering if I could come around and talk sometime," Eddie said. "Not about church or god or religion. I just need someone to listen and maybe give me a reality check every once in a while. Between a relationship, buying this place and getting shot at, sometimes I have no idea what I'm doing."

"My life is devoted to talking for an hour on Sunday morning and listening the rest of the time," Dom said. "I'd love to visit with you whenever you like. You could come by on Tuesday morning again so we have the place to ourselves."

"I'd like that," Eddie said. "I'd like that.

CHAPTER 40

The room in San Antonio was dark, no overhead lights were on and there were no windows. It was still two hours until dawn. Eddie and Gus sat on the left side of the U-shaped table, a pitcher of water and small plastic disposable cups in front of them.

"The Bureau spares no expense," Eddie poured water into one of the cups.

"You'll be billed for that," Gus said.

"I'll drink slowly," Eddie said. "What do you know about the operation?"

"Not much more than you," Gus said. "Ben Olson called me late last night and told me they were moving in on the handler this morning."

"Have they had eyes on him?" Eddie said.

"No," Gus said. "A team of agents has been working with the Royal Canadian Mounted Police to keep surveillance on the house ever since we lost Driscoll. They've seen no one enter or leave the house."

"It's been almost three months," Eddie said. "No grocery store runs? Nothing?"

"Nothing," Gus said. "Regular deliveries, including groceries. Whoever this is does not like to leave home."

"They interview any of the delivery truck drivers?" Eddie said.

"They did," Gus said. "The drivers never see anyone. They leave boxes inside the screen door."

"Why did they wait so long to act?" Eddie said.

"Red tape, pure and simple," Gus said. "Getting approval to send FBI SWAT in required a lot of talks between Ottawa and D.C."

"But, it's Canada," Eddie said. "Aren't they like a state now?"

Three more men and a woman walked in, the door closed behind them and the red safety light came on as the security systems were set in place.

"Gus, it's good to see you," Special Agent in Charge Holloway said. "I keep expecting to get a call from

Hoover that you're replacing me."

"That would be news to me, but when you're ready to move on I'll definitely consider it," Gus said.

"So what can you tell me about this?" Holloway said.

"I know you've been briefed on the suspect Aran Driscoll, and you know about his activities in Austin three months ago," Gus said. "DC has been working on intel about his possible handler. They've just received clearance and are moving on the handler this morning."

"Sounds good," Holloway said. "And Eddie, you healing up?"

"Slowly," Eddie said.

A cellphone vibrated in front of Holloway and he glanced at the message.

"They're ready," he said.

One of the other men brought the images up on the four flat screen televisions mounted on the wall.

"Not as fancy as what you're used to from the JTTF, I'm sure," Holloway said.

"Functional outweighs fancy every time," Eddie said.

The sound from the SWAT team came through the speakers. Eddie, Gus and Holloway pulled on headphones with microphones that came around in front of their mouths. For a moment Eddie thought of the similar room back in Virginia, watching the large screens as Clem Akins and his Rangers were sent in to a trap in Afghanistan. A mine had taken Clem's leg off and killed several of his men.

"This is Olson," a voice came through. "Teams are in place."

"Ben, how the hell did they get you out there?" Eddie said. "I thought you were driving a desk to retirement."

"I was bored stiff and getting fat off the shitty cafeteria food at Hoover. I volunteered to be out here," Ben Olson said.

"Glad to have you there," Eddie said.

Unmarked vans and cars with cameras were parked around the rural home near Essex, Canada. The images began to appear on the screens in front of them. It was still dark and the outline of the house was in infrared green.

"We're signaling SWAT now," Olson said. "We are a go."

Dark figures could be seen moving through the fields surrounding the two story farmhouse as the two dozen FBI SWAT team members approached the building.

"Entry team is preparing to breach," Olson said. "Is the perimeter secure?"

Voices from RCMP units at either end of the country road came through.

"We're clear from the east. Putting roadblock in place."

"Same from the west, all clear."

The screen lit up as the agents took the front door down with the heavy battering ram and the men entered the house, assault rifles raised as they dispersed into the building. The ring of agents surrounded the house and moved in closer to ensure the occupant didn't attempt to escape from one of the windows or the back door.

Radio transmissions from the entry team became audible through Ben Olson's microphone into the room in San Antonio.

"Clear, clear, clear," they continued to hear in the background as the rooms were checked and Olson entered the house.

"Doesn't make sense," Gus said. "Nobody's come or gone for over two months. Gotta be someone in there."

"Clear, clear," more voices came. "Ground floor cleared."

"Do we have a bird in the air?" Eddie said.

"We have air support from an RCMP chopper holding out of audible range," Olson said.

"Doesn't matter if anyone hears the chopper now. Does it have infrared?" Eddie stood and went to the screen showing the satellite view of the house. "Get it in there to check the fields."

"Top floor clear," Olson said. "Awaiting word on the basement."

"Where the hell is he?" Gus said.

"Ben, can you connect the pilot's radio," Eddie said.

"One second," Ben said. "Okay, you should have two way communication directly with Chopper One now."

"Thanks," Eddie said. "Chopper One, go in low and look for any small outbuildings, sheds, anything."

"Understood," the helicopter pilot said.

The shadow of the helicopter came across the satellite view of the property on the bottom left screen then moved north toward the pasture behind the house.

The SWAT team was conducting a second sweep of the house as more agents entered the building to begin a detailed search.

"Agent Olson, there's something you should see in the basement," the lead SWAT agent lead him to the small door that opened to the stairs.

"Headed downstairs, Eddie," Olson said. "Switching on my camera."

One of the screens on the wall changed from the external view to the camera mounted on Ben Olson's bulletproof vest. They saw the tight, dark stairwell down to the lowest level of the old house. Once at the bottom

Olson followed the man until they reached another door. The SWAT team had removed it from its hinges to bypass the lock.

"We have at least 30 cellphones, all laid out on tables. Each phone has a notepad beside it which appears to have details about every message sent and received including dates and names," Olson said.

Olson moved the camera back and forth at the tables to give Eddie, Gus and the rest of the agents in San Antonio a better look.

"Then up here on the walls are whiteboards with what looks like initials, more dates, and who knows what else," Olson said as he continued to scan the room.

"Stop there," Eddie said. "Go back a little."

The image paused then moved back to the left as Ben followed Eddie's instructions.

"Right there, it says H.C." Eddie said. "That's probably Hector Castellano, the soldier from Redstone."

"What's written under there?" Gus said.

Olson moved the camera slowly down the list on the wall in front of him.

"Looks like a shopping list for a terrorist," Olson said. "C4, sniper rifles, handguns, knives."

"This is Chopper One. We found something," the pilot said. "Can we get some people to check this out?"

The men all looked at the view from the helicopter's high-resolution camera. The sun was beginning to come up and the pictures were changing from green toned night vision to dark reds and browns. In the middle of a field a hundred yards away from the house was a small shed.

"Looks like an irrigation and fertilizer shed for the fields," Holloway said. "I grew up on a ranch in Montana, we had one just like that."

A dozen members of the SWAT team began to circle the shed, moving slowly through the overgrowth left from years of the fields not being tended to.

"We have a heat signature," the pilot said.

"Inside the shed?" Holloway said.

"Negative, the shed is cold," the pilot said. "About sixty yards northwest of the shed."

"Use extreme caution," Holloway said into his microphone. "Subject is likely armed."

"Understood," the SWAT team changed directions.

The men moved quickly from the outbuilding and worked their way through the field.

"40 yards out," the pilot tracked the agent's progress towards the subject. "Thirty yards out."

"We have visual on camera," Holloway said.

They could see the shape of the body as it moved

through the field, still shrouded in shadows from the low ridgeline to the east.

The agents on the ends of the line moved out ahead to form a half circle to begin to surround the subject.

"20 yards," the pilot said. "Subject has stopped and is in prone position, hands on head."

"We have visual on the ground," the SWAT team closed in on the subject, M4 assault rifles aimed.

On the camera they saw as the first two agents reached the subject. One man put his knee down on the subject's back as another pulled a zip tie restraint to the wrists. They raised the person up to their feet and checked for weapons.

"Is that…" Eddie said. "Is that what I think?"

"Subject is in custody and is clear of any weapons," came from the radio on the ground.

"Chopper One, can you zoom in?" Holloway said.

The image moved quickly as the lens adjusted and refocused on the person in custody.

"It's a woman," Eddie said.

CHAPTER 41

S WAT transported the woman by armored van to the RCMP station in Tecumseh, just across the river from Detroit, until paperwork could be filed to extradite her to the states.

"Sent photos and prints to you," Olson said. "You'll probably get them run faster than the Mounties."

"Received and running now," Holloway said.

The men were back in the sealed room in San Antonio after waiting an hour for the suspect to be secured.

"What we have is a woman in her early to mid-sixties," Olson said. "French accent. No identification on her but we found a stockpile of passports in the house, each with a different name."

"Was there a French passport?" Gus said.

Olson flipped through the pile of evidence with his rubber-gloved hands.

"Indeed there is," he said. "Name on it is Pauline Delles. Still could be fake."

"It's something to start with while prints and facial recognition get going," Holloway said.

"She say anything?" Eddie said.

"She asked for hot water with lemon," Olson said. "And has been chatting with a couple of the French speaking Mounties. She seems very polite. Not very terrorist like."

"There you go geriatric profiling again, Olson," Eddie said.

"We got a hit on the name," Holloway said. "Paulina Delles, born 1951 in Pontarlier, France. Last known record of her was in 2007."

"Age fits, language too," Gus said. "But what's the connection?"

"Just got word from the forensics team still at the house," Olson said. "They found access to a tunnel from the basement. It was hidden behind one of the whiteboards that was hinged to the wall. The tunnel runs from the basement to the shed."

"Sneaky old lady," Eddie said. "Any sign of anyone else living in the house?"

"Negative," Olson said. "One bed, toiletries for one, only a few plates and glasses. And she's not that old. I'm only a few years younger than her, thank you."

"Olson, you going in?" Eddie said.

"Yup, headed in now," Olson said.

They watched the screen with the interrogation room and saw Ben Olson walk in through the door behind the woman. An RCMP officer stood inside the room and locked and blocked the door after closing it.

"My name is Ben Olson," he said. "I'm with the United States Federal Bureau of Investigation."

The woman nodded.

"Do you understand English well enough to continue?" Olson said.

Another nod.

"Do you know why you are here?" Olson said.

The woman nodded again.

"Do you know Aran Driscoll?" Olson said.

She looked down at her hands.

"I do," her French accent was strong.

"How do you know him?" Olson said.

"I've never met him," she said. "I only communicate

with him through email and text messages."

"What is the nature of the communications you have with him?" Olson said.

"I assist him in his job," she said.

"What kind of assistance," Olson said.

She looked up at Olson and locked eyes with him.

"I locate and provide weapons and explosives, identify and use other assets to coerce individuals to carry out tasks for him and arrange travel through safe channels when needed."

"Okay," Ben said. "I appreciate your being so helpful. What kind of work does Aran Driscoll do?"

"He's a mercenary, an assassin," she said. "He kills for money."

Eddie and Gus leaned back in their chairs.

"This is unexpected," Eddie said. "Who'd have thought she'd give everything up so easily?"

Ben Olson continued.

"Do you know where Aran Driscoll is now?"

She smiled at Ben and picked up her cup of hot water with lemon and raised it to her lips. She tilted her head to the right and closed her eyes as she ground her teeth together then straightened up and drank her water and set it down.

Eddie stood up. "Get a paramedic in there now!"

"What? Why?" Gus said.

"She just swallowed something," Eddie said. "Olson, she just poisoned herself."

They saw Ben put his hand to his ear as he listened to what Eddie was saying.

"I don't have long," she said. "This is a better way to go than if I let him do it, which he will."

"Who?" Olson said. "Driscoll?"

He rushed around the table to her as she began to slump in the chair. "What did you take?"

"Geneva," she said. "William White. Search the house, you'll find everything you need. Please kill William White for me."

She fell to her right into Ben Olson's arms as two medics came in through the door. They moved her to the floor. One man worked to open her airway as the other checked pulse.

"Airway is completely swollen and blocked," the medic said. "No pulse."

They sat back on their heels from their kneeling positions on either side of the woman.

"What the fuck," Eddie said. "Did we really just see that?"

"We did," Gus had his head in his hands.

CHAPTER 42

"I've got something you need to see," Gus's voice came through the phone.

"I don't even feel like getting out of bed much less seeing anything," Eddie said. "I worked a late concert last night."

"Trust me, you want to see this," Gus said. "Get to the office as fast as you can."

The phone went dead.

Eddie got out of bed and went into his bathroom and looked in the mirror. It had been three months since the shooting and his face showed no signs of the fight. He ran his hands across his chest and traced the outlines of the bullet holes that had been stitched up. He put pressure on his ribs and felt only soreness and no real pain.

He took a short shower then dressed and picked his favorite porkpie hat, and left the apartment. The rental Impala had been turned in while he was in the hospital. Part of the business he had bought from Buddy's family included a twelve-year-old Ford F-150 king cab pickup.

Eddie turned onto Research Boulevard and glanced over at the former FBI office. Half the building had been deconstructed and was just now beginning to be put back together with reinforced materials. The satellite field office had temporarily moved two buildings down to an older construction four-story office until their space was ready for them again. He found Gus in his cramped corner office.

"Coffee?" Gus said.

Eddie nodded.

"Couldn't you have just told me over the phone?" Eddie said.

"Nah, you needed to see this in person," Gus said.

"So what's so important," Eddie said.

Gus pulled up a series of photos on the large LCD screen that took up most of his desk. The images were black and white and blurry from being zoomed in on but they were unmistakable. Eddie leaned forward.

"How did you…" Eddie said.

"I used my new best friend in DC," Gus said. "Ben Olson has been leading an official task force out of DC. He got access to all of the FAA footage from every possible airport Aran Driscoll would have flown through, from the day he disappeared, and has had a dozen new agents going through every second of each tape."

"You called in your favor with the Director?" Eddie said.

"This asshole blew up my building, killed one of my agents, put you and me in the hospital," Gus said. "Hell yeah I called in my favor. I have sixteen people in DC going through more footage in a week than we could in a year."

They stared at the images, a lean man in jeans, a black long sleeve shirt and his right arm in a sling. The progression of photos showed him in the waiting area of an airport gate, handing his ticket to the boarding agent, and then he disappeared onto the jetway.

"Holy shit," Eddie said. "When?"

"Five days ago," Gus said. "Pretty brilliant. He waited us out until he didn't think we wouldn't be looking anymore. Who would have thought that a terrorist would hang out for 12 weeks rather than get out of the country as fast as possible?"

"He's had plenty of time to heal but he's still in a sling," Eddie said. "Taking his handler down must have broken his line of communication to get medical help."

"If you hadn't gotten that bullet in him he could have walked into any hospital and been treated, no questions asked," Gus said. "But hospitals are required to report all gunshot wounds to the police. So instead he's been hiding out with a bum wing."

"What airline? What flight?" Eddie said.

"McCarran International in Las Vegas. The flight connected through Miami then to Dublin."

"Did he connect to anywhere in Dublin?" Eddie said.

"We don't know," Gus said. "Our access is limited to U.S. airports. We've been through the passenger manifests for both flights here and only three names match up. None are Aran Driscoll."

"I wouldn't expect him to use his real name," Eddie said. "Have you cross checked the three names against real people?"

"No, this is my first day as a federal agent," Gus said. "Of course I did. It appears he was travelling as Miles Shaughnessy. The other two names checked out and were cleared."

"So we don't know where he went from Dublin?" Eddie said.

"I'm working any friendlies I have at State to get a contact with the Irish Garda, but so far no luck," Gus said.

"How about the NSA?" Eddie said. "Can't we get into their system?"

"I wish I could," Gus said. "But ever since Snowden they're locked up tight and not sharing a damn thing."

"Okay, well, let's assume he didn't take another flight from Dublin. Ireland isn't that large a country," Eddie said. "He might have rented a car at the airport."

"Even if he did it likely was with a different name than he flew with," Gus said. "I've done a little research. There are nine car rental agencies at Dublin airport. Three require pre-booking, which he wouldn't do, so that leaves six. Three of those are headquartered in the U.S."

"He wouldn't have used any of those, he'd know we could access their records too quickly," Eddie said.

Eddie pulled up the list of car rental agencies at the Dublin airport.

"We could try calling each one, see if we get anywhere," Gus said.

"Too impersonal," Eddie said. "No one in another

country is going to give business information to the FBI over the phone."

Eddie leaned back, put his hands behind his head and looked at the stained drop-tile ceiling.

"I know that that look," Gus said.

"I'm going to Ireland," Eddie said.

CHAPTER 43

The cinder block building looked as drab as it always did. The original white paint had been covered with a shade of taupe years ago and that paint had faded into a color with no name. Eddie and Eva sat in her car as he stared out the window towards the former hospital turned nursing home.

"When will you be back?" Eva said.

"When it's done. I'm hoping it won't take long," Eddie said.

"Can Gus go with you?" Eva said.

"Not this time. He needs deniability over anything that happens," Eddie said. "State Department would have his head if he was involved in an overseas operation without permission."

Eddie heard Eva hold her breath and exhale slowly through her nose.

"Are you going to kill him?" Eva said.

He thought about the question and about whom it was coming from. She didn't know what he was capable of, the work he'd done early on with the Bureau and the task force.

"I don't know," Eddie said.

The conversation faded away with the uncertainty of the answer. She reached over and took his hand in hers.

"You sure you want to do this," Eddie said. "We can still head downtown for margaritas. I have a few hours before my flight."

"Yes, I'm sure," Eva said. "He's your father, of course I want to meet him."

"But it isn't really him," Eddie said. "Not the father I grew up with. Though in a way I guess that's a good thing."

"Why's that?" Eva said.

"Growing up in James Holland's house was never easy," Eddie said. "At least not for me. Shelley had a different experience. From birth I was expected to follow him into the army, become a Ranger."

"And you never wanted that?" Eva said.

"I told myself I did for a long time but as I got older, into high school, I knew I wanted to work for the FBI,"

"Did you ever try to talk to him about it?" Eva said.

"He wouldn't listen, but I probably didn't make it easy on him either," Eddie said. "When I was like twelve and thirteen the only thing I ever said to him was 'I don't know.' We fought constantly. I had no idea how to act around him, what to say to him. It just resulted in a lot of yelling."

"What about after your mother died?" Eva said.

"That's when things got a little bit better because he just stopped talking at all," Eddie said. "He was never home."

"Did you two ever make peace before he came here?" Eva said.

"Nah," Eddie said. "No new posting or promotion meant anything to him. It was Ranger or nothing. I'm sure he's embarrassed of me now, leaving the bureau to find stalkers and catch cheating husbands in the act."

Eva leaned over and rested her head on his shoulder.

"You've done so much more than that," she said.

"But I keep coming, and just keep talking to him," Eddie said. "I guess it's cheaper than therapy."

"And far more convenient for you since he never

speaks back to you," Eva said.

"I'm sure he's thinking it inside there somewhere," Eddie said.

They exited the small car and walked through the parking lot and into the building, up the elevator and down the hall. Eddie paused at the closed door to his father's room.

"Margaritas?"

"No," Eva said.

Eddie pushed the door open. His father was where he always was, sitting in his chair looking out the window. The bed had been made earlier in the day by one of the staff. The heat was on high.

"Dad, it's Eddie." Eddie pulled the other chair over and sat next to his father.

"I want you to meet someone," Eddie said. "This is Eva. I was telling you about her."

Eddie stood and let Eva sit beside his father.

"Mr. Holland," she said. "I'm Eva."

She picked up his left hand and held it between hers.

"Your son is a wonderful man, you should be very proud of him," she said. "And your daughter Shelley is kind and caring and a great mother."

She gently squeezed his hand as she spoke.

"Eddie tells me you're an Army Ranger," she said.

"My father was a Marine."

She kept her sentences short and kept contact with his hand. Eddie sat on the edge of the bed and watched Eva interact with his father.

After half an hour of Eva talking to James Holland, they said goodbye and left the room.

"You know there are medications," Eva said. "Drugs that might pull him out of this state, even if only for a few minutes."

"They're all experimental," Eddie said.

"But he's in there. He hears you talk to him, knows when you are beside him," Eva said. "Don't you think he'd like to say something to you at least one more time?"

"Honestly I'm not sure," Eddie said. "He barely spoke when he could. He's not a man who says 'I love you' or 'I'm proud of you.' The only positive reinforcement I got from him was if he didn't complain about what I was doing."

"I have friends in research at the university if you change your mind," Eva said.

"I won't," Eddie said.

CHAPTER 44

E ddie walked off the Air Lingus plane into the terminal in Dublin. He had a small carry on bag and hadn't checked luggage. He headed towards the car rental agencies after quickly clearing customs.

The first rental booth was a large Europe-based rental agency and he walked past it, feeling Aran Driscoll would go with something smaller. The two remaining companies on his list were Dooley Car Rentals and Shamrock Transportation. He chose Dooley and waited on line until a young woman with a thick Irish accent called him forward.

"Good morning, do you have a reservation?"

"No, I don't," Eddie said. "I have a few questions."

"My pleasure," the desk agent said.

"I'm trying to find a man who may have come through here seven days ago."

Eddie produced a photo of Aran Driscoll from the airport surveillance and showed the woman.

"He'd have been wearing a black long sleeve shirt and had an arm in a sling," Eddie said.

She looked at the photograph and shook her head.

"A week ago," she said. "I was on holiday last week, but let me check with some of the others."

She stepped away from the counter and talked with two other rental agents sitting at desks behind her. A man stood and came up to him.

"Sorry, nobody recalls the man you're looking for," he said.

"Thanks," Eddie walked across the hallway to Shamrock Transportation and began again.

"Seven days ago?" the man's nametag said Patrick. "I don't remember anything. We had some craziness a few days ago, but I don't remember a man in a sling."

"How was it crazy? Extra busy?" Eddie said.

"No. We had an older couple from Canada rent a car," Patrick said. "The car was stolen from a petrol station just a few minutes after they left here."

"When did they rent the car?" Eddie said.

Patrick stood with a blank look for several moments. "Shite. It was a week ago now."

Eddie perked up. "Was the car recovered?"

"I don't know, they haven't told us if it has at least," Patrick said. "We've had a ton of paperwork because of it."

"My condolences on the paperwork," Eddie said. "You know what car they had?"

"Sure, it was a Ford Ka," Patrick said.

"Ka?" Eddie said.

"Yes, sir. Ka," Patrick said.

"Okay. I'm going to give you my cellphone number," Eddie said. "If any information about the Ka comes in, would you give me a call?"

"I'll do my best, sir," Patrick said. "Will you be needing a car today?"

"Yes, I will," Eddie said.

Eddie left the desk minutes later with the key to a tiny rental car and found his way out of the terminal. He negotiated the large roundabout just outside the airport from the wrong side of the road and shifting with his left hand. He followed directions on his phone that Gus had sent him, to the M50 west then exit after a few miles. He pulled into a shopping center and drove to the furthest corner of the lot that faced right back to the highway he'd just left, backed into a parking space and waited.

It was 20 minutes before he saw the green Jaguar drive into the parking lot then finally pull up next to his micro rental. The driver's window buzzed down and Eddie cranked his window until it was open.

"You Eddie?" the man driving the Jaguar said. He had an Irish accent.

"I am," Eddie said.

The man looked in his rearview mirror then out the passenger side window of his car then produced a small black bag from his lap and handed it through the open windows to Eddie.

"When you're done with it make sure nobody finds it again," the man said.

"Understood," Eddie said.

"Tell Gus he owes me," the man said. The window began to roll up as the sleek sedan backed up and drove back through the parking lot and disappeared behind the side of the building onto the road.

Eddie unzipped the small bag and found the black Glock 9mm pistol with three full magazines of ammunition. He took one mag and slid it into the grip of the weapon until it clicked then put the other two into the center armrest of the car.

"There are some things I don't know about Gus,"

Eddie said.

Back on the highway Eddie headed west on the M50 to the M3 highway then headed northwest, based only on the thought of Aran being from Northern Ireland.

He'd driven for an hour when his cellphone rang and he answered.

"This is Patrick, from Shamrock Transportation," the voice said.

"Patrick," Eddie said. "What's up?"

"I couldn't say any more while you were standing at the counter," Patrick said. "We're not supposed to talk to people about stuff like this."

"Okay, what is it?" Eddie said.

"All our cars have GPS tracking systems," Patrick said. "In case they get stolen."

"Do you know where the Ford Ka is then?" Eddie said.

"No, not now, but the tracker was active for about an hour after it was rented then our offices lost the signal," Patrick said. "The company tends to let stolen cars disappear rather than try to track them down, that way insurance pays for a new car instead of just fixing any damage."

"Where did the tracker go dead?" Eddie said.

"Just off the M6," Patrick said. "Near Kilbeggan."

"Patrick, thank you," Eddie said. "I owe you one."

Eddie stopped on the side of the highway and opened up the map from the rental agency. Then he pulled back into traffic, took the next exit and headed back the other way on the M3 then exited and headed southwest on the N52 towards the M6 and Kilbeggan, Ireland.

CHAPTER 45

T he countryside rolled by. He wished he wasn't on a manhunt and had Eva beside him to enjoy the views. He pulled into Kilbeggan and drove down the sleepy central street then parked in front of a pub and went in.

"Guinness," he said. He took a seat at the bar.

His beer came and he sipped it slowly, no idea how much longer he'd be driving that day.

"Anytin' else for ya'?" the bartender said.

"Yes sir," Eddie said. "Have you seen this man?"

He showed the photograph of Aran Driscoll at the airport in Las Vegas.

"No," the man said. "Should I?"

"Not necessarily," Eddie said. "Last I heard he was around here about a week ago."

"A week ago?" the bartender said. He turned to another man sitting at the end of the bar, a full beer in front of him and an empty glass beside it. "When was that car fire?"

"Car fire?" Eddie said.

"Not much happens around here, so it was big news," the man said. "Hell, most of the shops shut down to go watch it burn."

"What kind of car was it?" Eddie said.

"A Ford I believe," the man said.

"A Ka?" Eddie said.

"Perhaps," the man said. "They all look alike."

Eddie paid, thanked the man, and asked where the police station was.

"The station is just down the road but he's never there," the man said.

"Where would he be?" Eddie said.

The bartender turned back to the man at the end of the bar. "Sean, where's your brother?"

"Which one?" the drunk man said.

"Michael," the man said.

Eddie couldn't understand what the man said but the

bartender repeated it for him and Eddie left the bar. He drove through town until he saw the small grocery store the bartender had told him to look for. Just inside the front door of the store he found Michael Tarrant.

"Sure, the car fire," the officer said. His uniform was too big on his slim frame and the wide leather belt held no holster or weapon. "That was an excitin' day here."

"So I've heard," Eddie said. "Did you find anything in the car?"

"It was all pretty well burnt," the officer said.

Eddie thought through his limited knowledge of Aran Driscoll to think of anything the car might be able to tell him. He looked out the front window of the store and saw a bus parked at the far end of the lot. He turned back to the officer.

"That bus, does it stop here every day?" Eddie said.

The officer turned and looked at the bus.

"No, just twice a week," the officer said.

"When was the last time it was here then?" Eddie said.

"Oh, that would be, well, three days ago," the officer said.

"And before that?" Eddie said.

"Four days before that," Officer Tarrant said.

"What time was the car fire and what time does the

bus depart?" Eddie said.

"The fire was reported just about noon and the bus leaves somewhere around one o'clock."

"Thanks," Eddie ran out the door and through the small parking lot.

He got to the bus as a passenger was climbing on board. Looking in, the driver's seat was empty. Eddie leaned back against the bus and waited.

Ten minutes later a round man came walking through the parking lot from the store, a grey jacket that matched his grey pants and a hat that looked too small for his head. Eddie glanced at his watch, 1:20. The driver finally made it to the bus.

"Are you the American Michael said was looking for me?" the driver said.

"I am," Eddie said. "Have you seen this man, he might have been on the bus a week ago."

The driver looked at the photograph.

"If it weren't for the sling, I wouldn't recognize him," the driver said. "I keep to myself and drive the bus, but I remember seeing him in my mirror while driving. He kept rubbing that arm and his shoulder. He definitely looked like someone got the best of him."

"That was me," Eddie said. "I'd kind of like to continue where I left off. Where was the bus headed from here?"

"It keeps going west on the M6," the driver pointed in what seemed like a random direction.

"Do you remember where he got off?" Eddie said.

"I carried his bag off of the bus and handed it to him after he stepped down," the driver said. "It was in Ballyvaughan."

"Thank you," Eddie ran back towards his car.

The M6 runs west to the Atlantic across the middle of Ireland. Eddie checked the map before leaving then drove as fast as he felt he could get away with. The last thing he wanted was to get stopped with an illegal firearm in Ireland. An hour later he pulled off of the highway into the town.

It took an hour of stopping at pubs and shops showing the photograph of Aran Driscoll before someone recognized it.

Eddie stepped to the sidewalk and pressed the buttons on his phone to call Gus.

"What's up?"

"I need you to make some calls for me," Eddie said.

CHAPTER 46

T he small house in Ballyvaughan had smoke drifting
from the chimney, dissolving into the cold air
coming off of the Atlantic Ocean. Aran Driscoll sat
inside. He had patched his right shoulder up the best he
could do working with only his left hand three months
ago while sitting in a cash only motel far from the strip
in Las Vegas. He'd retrieved most of the nine-millimeter
shell Eddie Holland had put in him but some small parts
of metal were still inside, working to break free and
move their way through his body and infect his blood or
worse. The wound was still partly open more than three
months after the fight.

The sun had come up but there wasn't much more light coming through the windows on the overcast day. One lamp was on in the corner, which cast dull shadows across the room.

A slow knock sounded from the front door. Aran turned from his chair in the corner and looked.

"Aran, it's Eddie Holland," the voice came through the thick wood. "I'm coming in."

A moment later the front door opened and Eddie Holland stepped into the house with the Glock raised as he scanned the room until he saw Aran then closed the door behind him to block the cold air.

"Nice place," Eddie said.

"It's a shithole," Aran said.

"I was being nice," Eddie said. "You have a gun?"

"I don't," Aran said. "Besides, my shooting arm is in rough shape."

"Don't you have people who can help you?" Eddie said. "A handler?"

"You're a funny man, Mr. Holland," Aran said. "Usually I would, but she went missing. You wouldn't know anytin' about that, would ya'?"

"What about your employer, William White?"

Aran looked surprised.

"I would applaud you if I could," Aran said. "I met

White only once. After the news of what happened in Texas I got a single message that I was not to contact them again. I was cut off. Even Pauline wouldn't help me and she eventually stopped responding, so I can only guess you found her."

"They don't condone personal vendettas?" Eddie said.

"They have no problem with them, they just have a problem with me failing. Not good for business."

Eddie walked across the room and sat in the chair facing Aran. He kept the pistol on his leg, the barrel pointed towards Aran.

On the table beside the Irishman sat a bottle of Midleton Irish Whiskey. With his left arm he reached and poured a couple of inches of the brown liquid into a glass, picked the glass up and leaned forward. Eddie reached and took the glass from him. Aran Driscoll picked up the bottle.

"*Air do sláinte*," Aran raised the bottle in the air and gave the traditional toast for 'on your health.'

"*Sláinte agad-sa*," Eddie responded with the standard reply, 'health at yourself.'

Aran paused.

"You have some Irish in you?" Aran said.

"Long before the Hollands were Texans, we were Irish," Eddie said. "My ancestors came through Ellis

Island and changed their names from Holohan to Holland so they could get work."

Eddie took a sip on the smooth liquor while Aran took a long pull from the bottle.

"An Irish family is unlike any other kind of family," Aran said. "Do you have anyone left here?"

"Not that I know of. My father wasn't much on the past," Eddie said. "Heard a few stories from my grandmother before she passed."

"Tis a shame," Aran said.

They sat in silence for some time before Aran spoke again.

"I grew up in this house," Aran said. "I slept on the cot under that window. My mother had the bedroom over there."

"Where's your mother now?" Eddie said.

"Dead," Aran said. "I came back here a year ago and found her not well. We spent almost every night sitting in these chairs, most of them quiet but she'd have these amazing lucid moments where she'd tell me stories about my Da."

Aran drank from the bottle then stared down through the hole at the liquid inside.

"She died while I was in Texas. No one noticed for over a week until a lady from the church came to bring her food. They'd already buried her behind the church when I got back."

"I'm sorry," Eddie said.

"After my father left she was torn up. Can't imagine how she was after I left at sixteen," Aran said. "Of course you know what happened to my father."

Eddie nodded.

"I tried to get him to quit, to retire," Aran said. "I saw him in London. He was staying at a fancy hotel on the river. We stood on the balcony and he was spittin' over the edge, 'hope that hits ya' in the feckin' eye' he was yellin'. All those years later, he never forgave the Brits."

"He wouldn't quit?" Eddie said.

Aran shook his head.

"He had nowhere else to be. After London he went back to the desert. It was maybe a month later when the bombs dropped on him."

The two men stared at each other. Aran raised the bottle to his lips again and the liquid inside sloshed as he drank. He lowered the bottle and set it back on the table beside him, the whiskey now half gone. His fingers ran down the side of the bottle, almost caressing it.

"I may miss this the most," Aran said.

Silence fell across the man again as the alcohol slowed him down. He'd spent most of the last week since returning to Ballyvaughan sitting in this chair, going through bottles to dull the pain in his arm. He turned to Eddie and looked him in the eyes.

"So, ya come to kill me?" Aran said.

"No," Eddie said. "I'm not going to kill you. That's not who I am or what I do. But if my bullet three months ago had hit you a few inches over and pierced your heart and you'd died there on the floor, I wouldn't have cried."

"But you've killed before," Aran said.

"Yes, I've killed before. But not like you," Eddie said. "Not close up, not without good reason, not for money."

"You'd watch a television screen as a drone flew over a desert village and dropped bombs on the people below," Aran said. "Men. Women. Children."

Eddie looked at his hands. The wounds from their fight were gone.

"We always did our best... I always did my best to ensure only our intended targets were in harm's way," Eddie said. "But there are mistakes."

"Mistakes," Aran said. "You sleep at night?"

"Sometimes I don't," Eddie said. "Are you condemning me for having killed? That seems more than a bit hypocritical."

"Perhaps," Aran said. "But I'm at peace with myself and with my God."

He adjusted himself in his chair and noticed Eddie move his hand closer to his gun.

"How does a contract killer claim to believe in God?" Eddie said. "Don't you violate about every page of the bible each time you step outside this house?"

"No," Aran said. "Only one commandment. And for that I've given my confession. So if you aren't here to kill me, what then, you going to arrest me? I don't have a gun. I can't fight back."

"I'm not going to arrest you either," Eddie said.

"Then what?" Aran said.

"There's some men outside. Men who'd like a word or two with you," Eddie said.

Aran's shoulders lowered and his eyes floated to the front door then back at Eddie. It was the first sign of weakness Eddie had seen in the man.

"Which men?" Aran said.

"There's a few from SIS," Eddie said. "Something about an incident on the Tube in London a few years back."

"Ahh, yes," Aran said. "That was my Da. Guess they'll take whichever Driscoll they can. They're still pretty mad about that one."

"Yes, they are," Eddie said. "Then after them are agents from three other countries. After all of them are done, if anything is left of you, you'll be shipped back to the United States where you'll be tried, convicted and put to death. But we really don't expect that to ever happen."

"I think you are probably right about that," Aran said.

"One more drink?" Eddie said.

Aran picked up the bottle and leaned forward and poured another shot into Eddie's glass. The two men drank then sat quietly.

"Okay," Eddie said. "It's time."

Aran looked calm as the door opened and two men in suits walked in followed by several armed agents from the British Secret Intelligence Service.

"Aran," Eddie said. "Your father and the rest of the men who died in that drone strike. They were responsible for recruiting children, ten and eleven year olds, to put on vests filled with explosives, nails and ball bearings. Those kids died and took dozens of other innocent people with them all in the name of a jihad your father didn't give a shit about. I ordered that drone strike and everyone above me signed off on it with no regrets when they read my report. That was work. It wasn't personal. If it hadn't been me, it would have been any number of other agents who received that intel and acted on it."

"I wish it had been. Maybe another man would have been easier to kill," Aran said.

"You came close," Eddie said.

"Tell me," Aran said. "Would you do something for me?"

"What," Eddie said.

"Bury me in Ballyvaughan," Aran Driscoll said. "My Ma's grave is here. I'd like to be with her."

Eddie looked at him and gave a slight nod.

"I'll see what I can do."

Aran tried to stand up. Eddie stood and helped him then Aran picked up the bottle of Midleton whiskey and pressed the cap back on. He held it up to see the liquid inside then reached out to hand it to Eddie.

"This shouldn't go to waste," Aran said.

Eddie took the bottle and walked across the room and through the open door and pulled it closed behind him. He walked past the rest of the British agents waiting outside the house to the car that waited for him.

CHAPTER 47

The small car sat in the middle of an old stone bridge over the River Shannon. Eddie leaned on the side looking out over the water while he talked on the phone.

"I'll be back soon, I promise. I just need some time," Eddie said. "That's not right. I want some time."

"I can't say I understand, but I can accept it," Eva said.

"It has nothing to do with us," Eddie said. "Without you I'd be lost."

"That I understand," Eva said.

"Love you," Eddie said.

He hung up the phone and put it in his pocket then looked either direction to make sure no cars were coming and reached under the back of his jacket and pulled out the Glock and looked at it.

"Such a shame," Eddie said.

He easily broke the weapon down into the individual pieces then dropped them off of the bridge into the deepest part of the river and watched until the circles created by the splashes had gone away. He picked up the bottle of Midleton from the low wall of the bridge and took a pull of whiskey then capped it and got back into the car.

Traffic was light as he made his way down through the country. He wanted to take the longer route through the towns along the southwest coast of Ireland but instead chose to take the direct route and save the scenic views for a trip with Eva.

He arrived in Kinsale after dark and found a bed and breakfast with a room available then walked into town for a beer before bed. He walked around the picturesque village the next morning and found a jewelry store. A man sat in the corner of the showroom at a cluttered workbench, crafting the items he sold.

"You the owner?" Eddie said.

"I am," the man said.

They spoke for half an hour about the jewelry, the village and Ireland.

"I need something for a lady," Eddie said.

The man looked at Eddie then stood and stepped through the faded curtain into the backroom then came back with a small box.

"I finished this one a few days ago," Pat said. "I wasn't sure if I was even going to sell it. It seemed too good to part with."

Eddie opened the box and held the small pendant in his palm, a hand crafted Irish symbol made out of silver. The symbol was clean and modern, not as round and traditional as the rest of the jewelry in the shop.

"The tourists all want the typical Irish symbols, all curvy and beveled," he said. "I'm so tired of making that shite, but it pays for me to keep this place open."

"It's perfect," Eddie said. He chose a simple silver chain to go with it and paid the man then asked for directions.

He walked a few blocks to the courthouse and talked to various people who helped him look through old books of records then left the building. He looked at the map he'd picked up at the bed and breakfast and began walking. It took only 20 minutes and he came to a stop in front of a small house, an Ireland flag with tattered edges hanging beside the front door.

Eddie went up the three steps to the door and knocked. A moment later the door opened to an older woman.

"And who are you?" she said.

"I'm Edward Holland," he said.

She tilted her head and looked at him.

"My great-great-grandfather was Edward Holohan," he said.

The woman smiled.

CHAPTER 48

E va Taylor held the pistol with both hands, her right forefinger extended across the trigger guard as she stared down the barrel. Even as the daughter of a Marine she had never aimed or even held a gun and the thought of pulling the trigger went against everything she thought she believed in. When she was a child she detested seeing her father clean his sidearm at the kitchen table.

The only cloud in the blue sky passed in front of the sun and the shadows on the ground faded away.

"Pull the trigger," Eddie said.

She brought her finger to the trigger and squeezed.

The slide flew backwards then forwards and loaded the next round. She pulled again to release another round then lowered the weapon, her body shaking.

"Oh my god," she said. "That was incredible."

Eddie reached out and took the weapon from her hands and checked the chamber to make sure it was clear.

"So why the sudden interest in shooting?" Eddie said.

"Well, I figured if I'm going to live in a house with guns, I should know how to use them," she said. "Especially with a guy around who tends to get shot at."

The words bounced through Eddie's head as he processed them several times to make sure he'd heard what he heard.

"Really?" Eddie said. "You sure you're ready?"

"I was sure I was ready when you asked me," Eva said. "I just wanted to make sure I thought about it first and didn't jump in too quickly. Plus a few things kinda got in the way the last few months."

"This is wonderful," Eddie said. "I can't wait to get your stuff moved into my apartment."

"I don't think so!" Eva said. "I know this is all just a ploy to have room for a larger television."

"I don't care about the TV, I'm thinking hot tub," Eddie said. "And maybe a pool table."

"Uh, no," Eva said. "Well, maybe a pool table."

He grabbed Eva to kiss her and she pushed him away.

"I'm here to shoot, buddy."

"Okay, okay," he said. "But let's try something different. Put your left foot forward and your right foot at a 45 degree angle, bend your knees slightly."

He handed the gun back to her then stepped in behind her, his body pressed against hers as he moved her into the Weaver stance, providing more stability for aiming and firing. He extended her right arm out in front of her body, her left arm bent and coming up under the gun for support.

"Getting a little close there, aren't you," she said.

"Just taking any opportunity possible," he said. "It's been a while since we made love."

"You mean this morning?" she said. "It hasn't even been three hours."

"That long?" he said.

After they finished shooting they drove back to her house in his Ford pickup. The CD player had Lyle Lovett's "Walk Through the Bottomland" coming through the speakers.

"You know there's music that didn't come from Texas, don't you?" Eva said.

"Sure," Eddie said. "It just isn't any good."

He pulled into her driveway and turned the engine off and turned to look at her.

"Want to come in and make up for lost time?" Eva said.

"Let me think about it… yes," Eddie said.